To Brodi

Great season.

Jonathan E. Pope
(aka Coach Pope)

MUZZ

by

Jonathan E. Pope

Check out muzzbook.com

Dedicated to my beautiful, loving wife, Libby, and my two wonderful children, Charlie and Liz. They are my inspirations!

Galaxy 9, System 7

INTRODUCTION

You remember that old question, "Are we alone in the universe?" Well, here in the year 2842, we know the answer to that question to be "Absolutely not!" In fact, it is now well documented that there are at least 11 galaxies, all with one or more planetary systems in them. Earth is located in Galaxy 5, formerly known as the Milky Way. Actually, Earth is a pretty popular place in the universe. I guess you could say it's kind of a "destination planet", a sort of a "melting pot", a place beings from other planets like to come to visit or vacation, and many times decide to move to. I think it has something to do with Earth's vast variety of climates and landscapes. You see, most the planets out there are more one way or the other; they're either hot or cold, they've got water or they've got sand, but Earth has a little bit of everything. If someone from the planet Gorna, in Galaxy 2, wants to snow ski, they can do that on Earth, then they can go to a beach and surf, then go mountain climbing, spelunking, hang gliding, desert dune buggy racing, and rain forest zip lining, all without leaving the galaxy or even the planet. And though we have the technology, there has been a big push intergalactically to keep Earth from getting "too modernized". Therefore, besides some light-speed spaceships and a bunch of aliens walking, or flying, or squirming around, Earth has remained pretty retro. Yeah, Earth is a pretty cool place, and that is where our story begins.

CHAPTER 1

THE STING

Vroom! Vroom! The dirt bikes revved, as the two teenagers glanced at each other both clutching their handlebars with their helmet clad heads pulled in low so as to make themselves more aerodynamic. The path in the woods ahead of them was worn. It was one they had ridden time and again, but never as fast as they were both preparing to go on this day. A little sibling rivalry can always take things to the next level, especially with a couple of daredevils like Charlie and Lizzie Paige. Even though, Charlie was her older brother, Lizzie had never backed down from a challenge from him in her life, especially a race. And the 15 year old could hold her own with a brother that was two years older, and pretty much great at everything he did.

"Ready!" Charlie yelled over the motors of the bikes. "Set!" He paused, giving one more glance and smirk to his sister.

"GO!" yelled Lizzie, before Charlie had a chance, and she burst out of her starting position like she'd been shot from a cannon, gaining the early lead. Charlie with a look of frustration tore out after her. The two of them sped through the forest passing large magnolias and pines, made a sharp left turn at the base of a hill with Lizzie still in the lead. The path was straight again for awhile and Charlie began to make up some ground. Toward the end of the straight away was a creek about seven feet wide with a slight rise to the ground as the riders approached. By this point the siblings were riding side by side, each with complete focus on the path ahead of them. No more glances and smirks. They reached the inclined bank of the creek in a dead heat and both left the ground at the same time and went sailing through the air. For the first time since the starting line, both riders smiled as gravity seemed to no longer have a hold on them, but instantly that freedom was gone as they both landed smoothly on the other side of the creek, and quickly got their bikes back up to full speed. The path had a slight right bend up ahead and was nearing the dead cedar tree, which the two had declared to be the finish line.

Lizzie, having known this right bend was coming, had positioned herself on the right side early in the race and had refused to give up this position as Charlie had gained his ground. As the two took the turn, Lizzie gained a slight lead, but then suddenly a squirrel darted across the worn path in front of Lizzie's bike. She quickly jerked her handlebars to keep from hitting the creature, but instead hit a dead log that lined the path. Her dirt bike stopped, but Lizzie did not, with the G-forces grabbing her and sending her over the handlebars and into a patch of wild growing dandelions, whose seeds burst like a puff of smoke as the teen landed on her back. Then Lizzie let out a delayed scream, and just lay there.

Charlie immediately, stopped his bike, tore off his helmet, and went running to his sister. As he reached her, he quickly, but carefully removed her helmet. "Lizzie?", he said frantically, "Are you okay? Did you hurt your back?"

"No, B.B.," she replied weakly (B.B. being her nick name for her 'Big Brother'). "My back is fine. I got stung."

"Stung?" Charlie replied confusedly. "You just flew like fourteen feet and landed on your back and you're worried about getting stung by

9

something?" He was unsure if he should be amazed at her toughness from the crash, or poke fun of her for her wimpy-ness from some little sting. "Well get up then," he said.

"I can't," she said even weaker and slower. "I… got… stung. In… my… bottom. I… got… stung." And with that last word, Lizzie passed out completely.

Charlie didn't understand what was going on, but he knew he needed to get his sister some help, so he went to pick her up off the ground, and as he rolled her over, he saw it. A bug. A big bug. A big dead bug, with a needle-like nose stuck firmly into his sister's fanny. He instinctively pulled the bug loose from his sister, and gave it a kick to put some distance between himself, his sister, and this strange, large bug, of which he had never seen the likes of before.

He hurriedly picked up his sister and put her onto his bike and sped away to the closest hospital.

Chapter 2

The Diagnosis

When he arrived at the local emergency room, Charlie just drove his bike through the automatic doors into the lobby and began yelling for someone to help him. Quickly, two men had Lizzie onto a gurney and were rushing her to see a doctor. Charlie followed them, ignoring the lady at the front desk, who was trying to get him to fill out some forms.

As they entered a room, another man approached and while pulling out a stethoscope and listening to Lizzie's heart, he asked, "What happened here?"

"Well, we were racing dirt bikes, and she wrecked ,and landed on her back, and..." Charlie began, but was interrupted by the doctor.

"Get her to radiology," he barked orders at the other two men, "I want a scan of her back and..."

"No. No." Charlie interrupted back. "She said her back didn't get hurt. Before she lost consciousness... she said her back wasn't hurt." The doctor and two male nurses waited. "She was stung. I don't know what kind of bug it was. I think it must have been alien. It was big, and..." Charlie was once again interrupted by the doctor barking orders, but this time with an even more serious tone to his voice.

"Get her to the sixth floor. Take her to Dr. Fox. Now!" he demanded. The doctor then turned to Charlie, "You go with them. She's going to need some information from you."

When the elevator reached the sixth floor the doors opened and Charlie read on the wall in front of him "Alien Medical Therapy". The two men wheeled Lizzie down a hall, stopping at an office and one of the men knocked on the frame of the already open door, which read "Dr. Addison Fox, Specialist in Alien Medicine". Before hearing a response from the knock, the man said, "Dr. Fox, Dr. Sherman sent us up with this case. He seemed to think it was pretty urgent."

A petite, pretty woman with porcelain like skin and dark hair who didn't look any older than twenty-one, rose behind her desk where she appeared to be skimming some type of medical journal while clicking a pen in one hand. She quickly set the journal down, clipped the pen to the inside of her shirt, and came to look at the patient. She took a flash light out of her white doctor's coat which was unbuttoned in the front, lifted one of Lizzie's eye lids and shined the light at her eye. She then did the same with the other one. Next she looked at the man who had spoken and said with a

British accent, "This girl's human. What is she doing up here?"

"Yes ma'am," the nurse said sheepishly, "Well, uh, well...he can tell you better," and he pointed to Charlie.

"Please do explain," said Dr. Fox to Charlie.

"She's my sister... and she was stung. I pulled out the bug that did it. It was big. Big as a basketball, w-well," he stuttered trying to be accurate with his description, "well not as round, but I'm pretty sure it was alien."

As he spoke he could tell he had gained the doctor's interest. And she said, "What's your name?"

"Charlie. Charlie Paige, ma'am. And this is my sister Lizzie."

"Well Charlie, this is very important. I need you to describe exactly what this 'big bug' looked like."

"Sure. It looked a lot like a big, foot wide ladybug, but instead of red it was kind of a shiny navy blue, and instead of black spots, it had kind of a yellow chevron pattern. And it's nose was like a needle, probably five inches long, I'd say." This description really seemed to peak the doc's interest.

"And where did you say your sister was when she got 'stung'?", Dr. Fox asked with intrigue.

"We were in the woods behind our house, riding dirt bikes; she wrecked and fell into a patch of...."

"Dandelions," Dr. Fox finished with a low, concerned voice.

"Yeah, that's right," Charlie said. "So you know this bug? Is it dangerous? Is she going to be alright? Can you help my sister, doc?"

"I know OF this bug. It's a Muzz Bug, and yes it can be very dangerous." She pulled Charlie into her office and grabbed her laptop computer. She typed in the phrase "Muzz Bug" and showed Charlie the picture of the big bug he had just seen in the woods behind his house. He read as Dr. Fox talked.

"Muzz Bugs are inherently a friendly species, which is one reason there is so little that is known about them. They rarely ever feel the need to attack. The last recorded incident of another species being stung by a Muzz Bug was about 800 years ago."

"This says they are from the planet Tropia in Galaxy 9, Planet System 7?" Charlie read.

"Yes, and I was unaware any had ever made it to Earth. This guy that stung your sister must have hitched a ride on a Tropian science mission, because none have ever been logged in through customs. And as I was saying, Muzz Bugs are named from the extremely poisonous venom each contains, called Muzz. It causes paralysis, within a minute of injection and will unfortunately kill its target in exactly 72 hours from the time of the sting if no anti-venom is given. That's 3 days."

"Anti-venom? So there's anti-venom. You have a cure?" Charlie exclaimed, clutching to hope.

"Well...not exactly," said Dr. Fox. "I'm not quite certain about this whole thing, but there is a legend about the anti-venom. I can't quite remember exactly. Oh, I really would like to confer with Professor Hootie at the university about all this."

"Who? What? What legend? Who is this Professor Hootie?" Charlie asked seemingly frustrated.

"Dr. Gordon Hootie. He is the head of the Department of Alien Sciences at the University of the Milky Way. He is THE foremost expert on alien history, geography, and languages, and it just so happens that his home planet is also in Galaxy 9, System 7. We should really go see him NOW. Your sister is stable, but the clock is ticking and in less than three days, we'll be too late. Look, Charlie, I will do everything in my power to help you save your sister, but we must hurry!"

Charlie looked down at his watch, and set a timer for 71 hours. **71:00:00.** His best guess was that it had been about 45 minutes since he'd heard his sister yell. The clock was now literally ticking.

CHAPTER 3

THE LEGEND

(71 HOURS LEFT)

Charlie followed Dr. Fox onto the hospital elevator. He was leery to leave his sister's side, but the doctor had assured him she was stable and he did not want to miss talking to Professor Hootie.

"So what's this guy like?" Charlie asked when they were on the elevator.

"Well, the Professor is an Aviottian, and he's quite nice...well, as long as you pay attention and do your reading."

"Avoittian? So he's like a bird-person?"

"I don't think they particularly like to be referred to as such, but yes, 'he's like a bird-person'," Dr. Fox responded.

Charlie had never actually met an Aviottian before. He'd seen them at beaches and malls, but never actually talked to one. His curiosity was rising on what information the professor might offer.

When the elevator reached the top floor, Dr. Fox swiftly stepped out and made a B-line down a hallway to some stairs. Charlie could barely keep up. This made him feel good at first because it made him realize that Dr. Fox really cared about saving his sister, but then panic followed from him beginning to grasp just how serious the situation was, and how time was such an issue.

At the top of the stairs they slung open a door and were on the roof of the hospital. Dr. Fox rushed to a small, two seater helicopter.

"Get in," she said, and Charlie did exactly as he was told. As soon as he was seated, safety straps automatically came over his shoulders and secured him into place. Dr. Fox had already cranked the chopper and before he could think, they were flying off the roof of the hospital.

Within five minutes, Dr. Fox and Charlie had landed on another rooftop, this of a very collegiate looking building at the University of the Milky Way. Charlie had been to the large university campus just a few months earlier on a tour. He was considering attending the prestigious college next year after he graduated from high school. The martial arts coach had offered the upcoming high school senior a full scholarship after seeing him win the Northern Hemisphere High School Championship back in the spring. Charlie was master level at tae kwon do, karate, jujitsu, judo, han mu do, and one of the newer martial arts, lin-do-bu, which was primarily done while standing on your hands.

The doc quickly unbuckled and raced to a door, and Charlie did the same. The two scurried down the college hallways and stairways with Charlie wondering if Dr. Fox even knew where she was going, but sure enough they opened a stairwell door, made a sharp right and there was a door to an office boasting the "Head of the Department of Alien Sciences, Dr. P. Gordon Hootie." They burst through the door to find an alien woman in a floral dress with green scaly skin, thick hot pink lips, and curly blonde hair staring at them.

"Can I help youuu?" the lady asked with a surprisingly southern drawl.

"We are looking for Professor Hootie," Dr. Fox replied. "It is of the upmost urgency."

"Oh, honey, he's teaching a class on Dialects of Galaxy 6 in room 302 right now," the professor's secretary informed them. Charlie and Dr. Fox both quickly turned and were almost through the door when the southern voice piped back up, "No. No. Now wait just a minute...Is it really after three o'clock? Well, giggle my gizzard, where does the time go? I'm sorry, sweetie, he's actually teaching a "Relics course" in lecture room 510 right now. I think he's talking about relics from Galaxy 2, System 2 today, but I just cain't be too sure. Sometimes he switches'em up on me you know, but that's just right down the hall from here." As the lady looked up from her computer screen she realized the two were already gone.

Within seconds, Dr. Fox and Charlie were standing at the top of a large lecture room, where Dr. Hootie was speaking. Dr. Fox did not hesitate in interrupting the lecture, which made Charlie slightly uncomfortable, yet he was glad she had done it.

"Professor Hootie. Could I have a word with you sir?" she announced.

Professor Hootie, who had been writing on a dry erase board facing away from the class, twisted his neck, turning only his owlish head around. He straighten his spectacles, and peered up toward where the voice had come from. He was a tall man. About six feet six inches was Charlie's guess. He was covered with orange, red, and yellow feathers, like beautiful fall foliage, with hints of brown outlining his face. His oval, golden glasses rested on his short yellow beak. A faint smile came across his face, as he then turned the rest of his body to match his head.

"Addison, is that you?" he asked with a tone to his voice of pure delight.

"Yes, sir, Professor, It's me."

"Class," he began, "let me have the pleasure to introduce Dr. Addison Fox to you all. She was a student of mine once. One of my best."

"Sir," Addison interrupted, "I need to speak with you. It's a very urgent matter, sir."

The smile left the professor's face as he realized something serious was going on. He nodded slightly to a teacher's aid in the front row and handed him the lecture notes. He looked back up toward the two intruders and said, "Meet me in my office."

It took only seconds for them to return to the professors office, but when they got there, he was already there seated at his desk. Charlie found it a little strange that his desk chair looked like a large bird's nest on wheels. The professor stared at them for a couple of seconds and then said, "So what kind of situation have we got here, Addison?"

She sighed and started, "This is Charlie. His sister was stung earlier today.....by a Muzz Bug."

"Where was she?" asked the professor. "Why would it sting her?"

Charlie had to jump in, "It was in the woods behind our house."

"Here on Earth?" the professor was obviously as surprised as Dr. Fox that a Muzz Bug had found it's way to Earth.

"Yes, sir," Charlie replied. "We were riding dirt bikes and she wrecked and landed in a patch of dandelions. Then it stung her."

"My boy, I doubt if it stung her as much as she just landed on it's nose. Muzz Bugs try not to sting if they can help it."

"Maybe it was just scared," Charlie said, "It got scared or angry and stung her?"

"Doubtful. You see, Muzz Bugs can typically only sting once. They die immediately after they sting something. The muzz ,that we consider 'venom', is actually a Muzz Bug's 'blood', and what we refer to as 'stinging', they would call 'transfusing'. These transfusions actually occur in half a second and remove the entire contents of muzz from a Muzz Bug's body. It's actually quite remarkable."

"But why did you say they 'typically only sting once'? If they die, isn't it pretty much always one sting and done? Maybe the one that stung my sister thought it was one of the 'multiple stingers'," Charlie debated.

"Muzz Bugs are quite honorable creatures," the professor's tone was that of great respect. "When I say they 'typically only sting once', I say this because if within one minute of them losing their muzz and dying, another Muzz Bug stings, or transfuses, the newly dead bug it can bring it back to life, but the other bug has now sacrificed it's life for the sake of the other. But the occurrence is not uncommon. A parent Muzz Bug, will quickly give its child a transfusion, or a mate to another mate, or even one sibling sacrificing itself for the other."

This statement brought tears to Charlie's eyes for the first time through this whirlwind of a day. His face turned toward the floor to try to hide them, and he spoke softly, "I'd do it. I'd switch places with her right now if I could."

The professor reached out and put his feathered wing-hand on the back of Charlie's head, "I know you would, my boy, I know you would." Professor Hootie then looked up at Addison and said, "You can count me in." Addison smiled.

This statement kind of startled Charlie back to life and he asked, "What do you mean? Count you in for what?"

"Son, we have to try to save your sister and I only know one way to go about doing that," the professor replied.

"The Legend," Charlie said quietly with confidence.

"That's right. The Legend of the Muzz Bug Anti-Venom," the Professor said trying to contain his excitement.

"So? What's the Legend?"

"They say that about 2,000 years ago a Muzz Bug himself found the anti-venom after he accidentally stung a creature of a different species and then immediately was saved by a transfusion from his father. The Muzz Bug said he would not let his father die in vain, and that there had to be a purpose for his death. It is said that the anti-venom was discovered in the Muzz Bug's own planetary system, that of Galaxy 9, System 7, which I believe has to be true since Muzz Bugs can only freely travel within their own system. You see, another remarkable fact about Muzz Bugs is that they can fly, not unlike the beings on my planet, but the remarkable part is that Muzz Bugs, can fly in outer space without any type of vehicle to carry them but only within their own planetary system. And though they fly at normal speeds while on a planet, the lack of atmosphere in space allows them to fly at extraordinary speeds, which essentially allows them to 'planet hop' to any of the twenty-two planets in Galaxy 9, System 7. But mostly they are very content on their own planet of Tropia and have very little reason to leave."

"The Legend says," he continued, "that after this particular Muzz Bug found the anti-venom he did not disclose it's location to anyone, in fear that somehow it might be used as a sort of 'pesticide' which could potentially wipe out his entire species. However, he did set up a series of clues throughout his planetary system which would ultimately lead to the anti-venom, in case an incident like this ever occurred again. To date, it has never been found, and although few have tried, the legend says it is a dangerous journey to undergo."

"Forget the clues, let's just go to all the planets and look for the anti-venom," declared Charlie.

The professor slightly chuckled at the youngster's ignorance. "My boy, there are twenty-two planets in that system. We would never have the time. Besides, we have no idea what it will look like. No idea if it is a solid, liquid, or gas. It could be Jell-O for all we know."

Charlie looked up at Dr. Fox who had been standing over him with her hand propped on the back of his chair, "So what's next then? Where do we start?" Addison nodded back toward Professor Hootie. Charlie turned his attention back to the owlish being.

"The Legend says that the original Muzz Bug gave the first clue to the Queen Muzz Bug, and that the clue has been passed along for generations to each succeeding queen. So, I'd say we need to head to the planet, Tropia, in Galaxy 9, System 7."

      "But first, we'll need a ship and a pilot," Dr. Fox chimed in, "And I think I know the fastest one."

CHAPTER 4

THE PILOT

(69.5 HOURS LEFT)

The three of them took the professor's classic 2150 Porche Terrapin RX8 convertible to speed away from the University. They only had to go about seven blocks until they reached "Arnie's Turn of the Millennium Arcade". Charlie knew this place. He used to come here a couple of years ago to play an interactive karate sparring game called "Foot Fist Fury". The arcade was a huge facility with over 900 games spanning the seven decades when video games were at their height from the 1980's to the 2040's. Charlie was curious why Dr. Fox was so intent on coming to this place. Mostly there were just a bunch on teenagers and slackers that hung out here.

When they arrived they went in through the main entrance. They passed kids of all species playing the early classics like Donkey Kong, Ms. Pac-Man, and Galaga. As they passed through the different decade rooms, Charlie saw Fronkites playing Golden Tee, a couple of Capritorts dueling in Dance Dance Revolution, and a human kid taking on a Quibert in a heated game of Call of Duty. He even passed his favorite, Foot Fist Fury, but was disappointed to find no one playing at the time.

They kept walking, rather briskly, to what Charlie perceived to be the back of the enormous gaming complex. They arrived at a door that posted a sign which read "RESTRICTED AREA", but Dr. Fox didn't hesitate to push the door open and continue her mission. They were now walking down a dimly lit corridor which to Charlie felt like the inside of giant aluminum can. They passed some metal lockers and then came to a door which was steel and locked. Dr. Fox knocked. A small window slid open about eye level on the door. A deep voice asked, "Can I help you?"

Dr. Fox inquired, "Jagger here?"

"Who wants to know?" asked the deep voice.

"Dr. Addison Fox," she said.

The deep voice paused, turned, then announced into the room,"There's a Dr. Fox looking for Jagger. Is Jagger here?" asked the voice as if he knew the answer but was giving someone the chance to hide if need be.

"Let'em in, Rosco," said a voice in the distance.

Almost immediately the large, heavy steel door creaked with movement and gave entry to the three visitors. As they entered, Charlie cased the place. Why had he never been back here? What was this place? And most importantly, why was he here now? As he surveyed the room, he noticed that all the machines were the same. They all looked like spaceship cockpits with 3D screens inside them, and they all read "Universe Space Racers". Charlie finally leaned in to Professor Hootie and asked in a whisper, "What is this place?"

The Professor replied, "Well my boy, this is essentially a training facility. Although, *some* of the beings here know they are training, and *some*," he paused, "some do not. You see, this 'game' is a complete, 100% accurate model of the universe and all its eleven galaxies. Actual pilots come here to stay on top of their skills, while some youngsters are allowed to 'play' as a recruitment tool...to see which ones have an aptitude for this sort of thing."

"So who's this Jagger?" Charlie asked.

Without saying anything, Professor Hootie raised his right wing-hand and pointed. Charlie's eyes followed the professor's point and he saw an ovalish image moving toward him in the dim lighting of the arcade. The being seemed to be moving in slow motion, but then Charlie realized it was just moving extremely slowly. It was a turtle-person complete with shell and everything. Most likely from Plantankia, in Galaxy 10, System 4.

"Great," thought Charlie, "Are you kidding me? This is 'the fastest pilot'? Really, a turtle?"

As he reached the three of them the turtle-man said rather quietly and slowly, "Hello there Dr. Fox. And to what do I owe the pleasure?"

Addison replied, also quietly, "We need a pilot. For a mission. A mission where time is of the upmost importance."

The turtle-man placed his hand on the small of the back of Dr. Fox, and guided her back toward the door through which they had entered. He said, "Maybe this would be best discussed outside." And all four beings walked, slower than Charlie would have liked, back through the heavy, steel door. As he was leaving, the turtle-man turned to the oafish looking creature wearing a black suit, with black tie, at the door and said, "Thanks Rosco. I think I'm done for the day," and he slipped him some money as they exited.

Once back outside, and alone in the corridor, Charlie, the professor, and Dr. Fox turned toward the the turtle-man who quickly released a couple of valves on each side of his shell. Each giving off a quick burst of air and puff of steam. The reptile-ish being tossed the now two pieces of shell off of his body, exposing a flight suit underneath along with a thin, fit frame. He turned to the wall which was lined with metal lockers, opened one, and hung up the two pieces of shell. Then he grabbed a pair of mirrored aviator sunglasses from a shelf in the locker, slammed the door shut, and did a smooth and swift pirouette. "Addy!" he said with a surfer like accent that had a touch of Texan to it, "What's this mission you're talking about?"

"Wait," interrupted Charlie. "What was all that? Where are you from? Who are you?"

"Well, bro. Which do you want to know first?" he replied.

"Ok, who are you?"

"I'm Jagger. And what name do you go by Mr. young interrogator dude?"

"This is Charlie," Addison answered for the boy.

"Well Chuck, like I said, I'm Jagger and I'm from the planet Conchu," he paused, then said, "Wait a minute, you didn't think I was from

Plantankia did you? Oh man, that's a whole system away from my home. Conchu is Galaxy 10, System 3. I don't know why you Earthlings get us confused." He paused again, then burst with a bit of laughter, "Nah, I'm just messing with you, dude. That's what I was going for. My disguise in there is that of a Plantankian. If those young pilots knew I was from Conchu, they might figure out who I was and I wouldn't get any training done. I'd be signing autographs all day. Not a bad get-up, though. Right? Bet you barely recognized me, huh, Addy?"

She smiled and said, "I recognized you just fine, and you shouldn't flatter yourself... talking about autographs. There's not a being for five galaxies who'd know who you were."

Jagger looked as if Dr. Fox had just completely popped his bubble, "Now come on, Addy, why you got to go and be like that?" he said sarcastically. "But seriously though, what do you three have going on, that you all need ol' Jagger here for?"

Addison spoke up first, "Charlie's sister was stung by a Muzz Bug earlier today and she is in complete paralysis."

"Muzz Bug? Never heard of it," said Jagger. "Will she be okay?"

The Professor chimed in, "If we don't find the anti-venom," he said, "the girl will die. And we only have 72 hours."

"Well really only about 70," stated Charlie looking at his watch. **70:22:23**

"So we need a ship and a fast pilot. That's where you come in," Dr. Fox said.

"Well giddy-up. I don't guess there's much else to say. I kind of owe you one, Addy, and anyway, a girl's life is at stake. So, what's the plan? Where we goin'? Where is this anti-venom?"

"Our first stop is Tropia," said Dr. Hootie. "It's in Galaxy..."

"Oh I know where it is," interrupted Jagger. "I may not have stopped at every planet in this universe, but I've flown by each of them probably three times at least. Galaxy 9, System 7. Lot of planets in that system."

"Yes there are," stated the professor who was visibly impressed.

"How big is your ship?" asked Addison. "I want to take the girl with us. I'm afraid if we do find the anti-venom we might not have time to get it back here to Earth. We should have her with us for time sake."

"We WILL find the anti-venom," exclaimed Charlie.

"My ship's big enough for the six of us," replied Jagger.

"Six?" asked Dr. Fox. "I'm only counting five, including Lizzie."

"Oh, yeah, well are you including Marvin?" Jagger asked matter of factly.

"Marvin? Who's Marvin?" replied Dr. Fox

"Marvin's my mechanic. Also kind of my co-pilot, first mate, little buddy. He's the Gilligan to my Skipper. Let's just say he's a good guy to have around. He's with the ship now over at the Washington Street hangar."

"Perfect," said Dr. Fox, "We'll go get the girl and meet you at the ship as quick as possible."

"Sounds good," replied Jagger, "I'll get on the horn and let Marvin know to get Lady Alabama ready for take off, and maybe I can swing by and pick up some beef jerky and Cheetos for the flight."

The two docs and Charlie climbed back into the professor's Porche Terrapin and sped back toward the hospital.

CHAPTER 5

THE SHIP

(69 HOURS LEFT)

The professor, Dr. Fox, and Charlie arrived at the hangar on Washington Street being chauffeured by the driver of the ambulance they were in, with Lizzie lying, as if peacefully sleeping, on a gurney in the back. Sirens whirling, they pulled into an area where a ship had its loading ramp open. The ship was sleek and white . It did not have wings or any visible propellors, but instead was rounded on the edges and pointed at the front, making it extremely aerodynamic. The shape of the ship reminded Charlie of a cyclist's helmet. And the ship was perfectly clean, like it had never been flown before. Charlie could see the distorted reflection of the ambulance in the shine of the ship as he peered out the window. He also saw a person of sort standing at the bottom of the ramp with a terry cloth wiping the side of the ship, like there was a spot he'd missed. This person was light-purple in color. He was shaped like a human, but had no hair, no eyes, no ears, or any other facial features other than a little rounded bump where you'd expect a nose to be. He was wearing a faded yellow mechanic's jump suit with the sleeves rolled up to his elbows. As Charlie stared at the being through the window, the lavender colored man looked back with his blank face and raised his right hand to welcome them.

The driver of the ambulance backed in toward the ramp and put the vehicle in park. All doors flew open as the occupants quickly emerged from the ambulance. Charlie helped the driver carefully remove the gurney with Lizzie on top, extend its taller rolling legs, and place them on the pavement below. As this was occurring, Jagger emerged onto the ramp from inside the ship.

"Stocked up on Cheetos," he announced light heartedly, but as he saw the girl lying there and was reminded of the severity of this mission, he quickly realized this wasn't the most appropriate thing to say. "Oh, sorry Charlie-dude, I didn't mean to..."

Charlie interrupted, "Hey man, don't apologize. This is the situation we're in, and we may as well make the best of it. I just want to thank you for being willing to come with us, and for letting us use your ship." Charlie smiled at Jagger, "Thank you, sir."

Jagger nodded and grinned, "Well hey, on that note, welcome to Lady Alabama. The fastest spaceship in this here universe....at least while I'm flying her."

The rest of the crew started walking up the ramp into the ship. The purple man excused the ambulance driver from pushing the gurney, and started following the others up the ramp. At about the mid-way point on the ramp, Jagger turned back to them and said, "Oh, did y'all meet Marvin?" and motioned his hand behind the others. Charlie, Addison, and Professor Hootie turned around to look at the lavender, bald, faceless man who was pushing Lizzie on the gurney, and when they did he stopped, stood up straight, raised both his hands and waved them in an excited, "glad to meet you" kind of way. But of course, this meant he was no longer holding the gurney, and the rolling bed, began rolling back toward him almost knocking him over, but he quickly regained control of it and once again began pushing it up the ramp.

"Marvin's from Chimbee Pank, in Galaxy 1, System 1," Jagger said. "He can't talk, because he's got no mouth, but he gets his point across, believe me, and he's the best mechanic I've ever met."

"Can he see and hear?" Charlie asked, since Marvin also appeared to have no eyes or ears.

"Well yeah," replied Jagger and gave a glance and a shrug to the professor like "what kind of question was that." "And he can also keep a beat," Jagger said and kind of smirked. Charlie looked at him confused. "You'll figure it out soon enough," Jagger assured him.

Once they were fully inside the ship, Charlie actually felt a jolt of excitement run through him. The cabin of the ship was open, empty, and clean with a everything being back lit by blue lights. The walls were lined with buttons, lights, and switches. Charlie could tell this craft was loaded with modern alien technology that had somewhat been banned from mainstream Earth life. He felt a little guilty about the sensation, but he'd never actually left Earth before and he could tell they were about to be embarking on a once in a lifetime adventure. He just hoped the adventure resulted in his sister being cured.

"Hey kid," Jagger addressed Charlie, "So what's the deal with your parents? Why aren't they here?"

Dr. Fox and Professor Hootie looked at each other as if to say, "Oh yeah, where are their parents?"

"Do they even know where you are? I haven't even seen you call them?" said Dr. Fox.

"Actually, they left a week ago on a month long space cruise to Galaxy 4. It's the first trip I can ever remember them taking, and I just don't want to worry them with this. Besides, what can they do? They're on a cruise ship with 10,000 other people, a galaxy away...it's not like they can just head back. I think it's best if we just get this situation handled and they can hear about it later."

"I hear ya bro," said Jagger, then he turned to Marvin who was finishing rolling Lizzie's gurney to the center of an area of the ship which had a circle of blue lights. He parked her gurney there. "Raise the ramp, Marvin," Jagger said. Marvin pushed a button on the wall which caused a holographic control panel to appear. He touched a few holographic icons and made a circle motion with his right hand. Immediately, the hydraulics of the ramp were put in motion and it began to rise. With a swipe of his left hand, Marvin shuffled through a couple more holographic screens until he found the one he was looking for. He again pressed a few buttons and with both hands turned palms up, he raised them like a maestro directing a symphony. With this motion the circle of blue lights surrounding the gurney brightened and you could almost see a clear energy coming from them and surrounding Lizzie's body. Marvin nodded to Dr. Fox, who at this point was closest to Lizzie. She then moved closer to her and Charlie watched with amazement as the doctor released the extended legs of the gurney, causing the bed to lower to the ground, yet Lizzie remained hovering in the same spot she had been, about chest high, like she was resting on the air.

"Well, Jagger," the professor spoke up, "I've been in many spaceships on my research missions, but never one like this. I am definitely impressed."

"Thanks, Doc. Yeah the Lady is pretty special alright. She's mainly built for speed, but has some other features you don't find on just any ol' ship. She's one of a kind my Lady is. Cuts travel times of your average light speed ships in half, and

I figure for this type of mission, that just might help." Then with a change in tone, he said, "So, how's about everyone takes their seats and we will get this bad girl in the air." Charlie kind of looked around to try to figure out where to sit as Marvin once again made some motions at the control panel and the floors lit up with the same blue lights he'd seen surrounding Lizzie. Jagger walked to the front of the ship and appeared to just sit it air. Reached up and pulled a steering apparatus down from over head. Charlie saw the professor and Dr. Fox find areas outlined in blue lights and they just sat down. He found an area himself and with some hesitation, sat, but when he did, the lights went off and he fell back onto the floor of the ship. The professor and Dr. Fox both tried to hold back from giggling but just couldn't quite seem to. Charlie flipped his head over toward Marvin who had both hands on his belly and his head shaking from his silent laughing. When Marvin saw Charlie looking at him he quickly stopped and immediately turned back toward the control panel.

Jagger said, "Ahh now Charlie, he's just having a little fun with the newbie. It *is* your first time space traveling isn't it?"

Charlie still on the floor, quickly turned his frustrated embarrassment into a grin and a little chuckle at himself. From on his back, he turned back toward Marvin and said, "Good one, Marvin." He then, with cat-like movements, placed his hands near his head on the floor, pushed off, and sprung easily to his feet in one swift movement. The others in the ship just kind of looked at each other like "who is this kid?" but none of them said a thing. Marvin brought the lights he'd cut off earlier, back up, and Charlie with confidence this time sat down in the invisible chair. Once he did, he also felt the energy, almost inflate and cover over his chest and lap as if snuggly and securely holding him into place.

Jagger, with a hologram control panel also at his reach touched a few "buttons" and with his right hand gave a downward pushing motion. A shield in the front of the ship lowered exposing a clear windshield and now everyone could see what was in front of them. Both Jagger and Marvin continued using the control pads and Charlie could feel the ship's engine come on, but it was the quietest, most gentle motor he'd ever heard or felt, especially compared to the dirt bike he had been riding just a few hours earlier.

The ship began to back out of the hanger, and once the nose was fully out, Jagger said, "Next stop, Tropia." And without even turning or getting a rolling start the ship lifted straight off the ground at a great speed, vibrating slightly as it rose, and a little more as it crossed through the Earth's atmosphere. Then once it was through, and was fully into space, the ship slowed and turned. Through the large windshield in the front of the ship, Charlie could see his home planet in a way he had never seen it before, and it was beautiful. The ship continued to turn and Earth left the viewing field and only a vast darkness of space, glittered with stars, lay ahead of them. When the nose of the ship got pointed to the correct setting, Jagger yelled, "Giddy up, little horsey!"

Charlie turned to look over his left shoulder at Marvin who swaying back and forth in has seat while beating on his chest like some kind of primitive ape. The ship then took off and the darkness in the windshield turned light.

The bright light quickly began to bother Charlie's eyes, and through his squinting he could tell the same was true for Dr. Fox and Professor Hootie sitting across from him. He again turned to look over his shoulder at Marvin, and saw him wearing sunglasses that pinched in on the side of his head, due to his lack of ears, and he was kind of dancing in his chair and Charlie could hear a low beat, going, "Nnt nnt nnt nnt," like the bass from a speaker, coming from the faceless man. Jagger, wearing his aviators, turned toward the squinting passengers and said drawing out his words, "Oooh, riiight. Sorry about that guys." And he used his control panel and the windshield quickly tinted, and the light dimmed and became bearable for the rest of the passengers. Marvin stopped his beat and his dancing and dropped his shoulders like he was sad that the light had gone away.

They rode like this for close to 9 hours. Traveling four galaxies away used to take days, but the newer ships had reduced that time drastically, and the Lady Alabama was the fastest of all. The crew, except for Marvin, decided to sleep during

Earth, but with more green land and not as much blue water.

Jagger steered the ship toward the planet and soon it was the only planet visible through the windshield. Jagger then said, "Hey Professor, how do I know where to go when we get down there?"

Professor Hootie asked, "Do you have a map on this ship?"

"Do we have a map?" Jagger said sarcastically. "Marvin, get the man a map."

Marvin used his holographic control pad once more, scanning and touching with his hands, then made a motion with both his hands like he was opening a book. With that motion a large 3D image of Tropia appeared in the center of the ship.

The professor still seated and secured into his seat once again looked at Jagger as if impressed and asked, "May I?"

Jagger realizing that the passengers had been sitting there the entire time quickly said, "Oh yeah, please. Feel free to move about the cabin as you'd like." Marvin did his thing and the "energy seat belts" released from the passengers. The three of them got out of their seats, all stretching a bit and walked over to the small, holographic planet floating in the middle of the room.

"The colors are remarkable," stated the professor, "which should help us find where we're going."

Charlie reached out to see if he could touch it, but his hand just went right through the image. The professor however, held his hands up, palms facing the image and moved them both to the right, and the image rotated like a globe on an axis. He rotated it again and again quickly. Up, down, left, right.

"What exactly are we looking for, Professor?" Dr. Fox asked.

"Come on, Addison, you should know the answer to that. You've taken my classes," Professor Hootie responded.

Dr. Fox thought for a second and then said one word. "White."

"Exactly," said the professor proudly.

"White?" Charlie asked quietly to himself while watching the ever moving image. All three of their sets of eyes were focused on the globe and Charlie screamed, "Stop! Right there! Right here! Look! Here's some white!" He pointed to an area on the image of the planet and the two doctors came to look from his point of view.

"Yes. Yes. That's it, my boy. Well done," the professor said. "That is the Forest of the Wimberlies, also known as Muzz Bugg Peninsula."

From the front of the ship they heard Jagger call out, "So will someone tell me where they want me to land this thing?"

At that point, Marvin squeezed his way between the three of them and the "globe". He pointed to the white peninsula and turned toward Dr. Hootie. The professor nodded and said, "Yes, that's the spot." Marvin turned back to the image and started up his bass noises, "Nnt nnt nnt nnt." He then made a frame with his hands, and put them in close to the white image and pulled them apart which caused the image to zoom in on the spot. Then he made a "scissors" with his fingers, stuck them into the holographic image and made a cutting motion. The white image separated from the rest of the globe and Marvin then put his hand behind the image and made a motion like a pitcher throwing a baseball in the direction of Jagger's seat. The image and coordinates of the location simultaneously popped up on Jagger's control panel monitor.

"Thanks, bro," they heard Jagger call out from the front. "We should be there in a few minutes now. You guys might want to take your seats again for the landing." And the passengers quickly complied with the ship's captain.

"You're going to want to land a little east of the forest," stated the professor. "Just aim for green."

"You got it, doc," replied Jagger and as they neared the location Charlie could see the image he'd just seen on the holographic globe, now coming into real life view through the windshield in front of him.

The ship lowered even more smoothly than it had taken off and it landed in the greenest field Charlie had ever laid eyes on. Marvin did his thing and the ramp's hydraulics were set in motion, lowering open. The crew wasted no time exiting the ship. Charlie looked around and saw the green fields once again. He also saw some animals in the distance that reminded him of dinosaurs, grazing on the grass. But it wasn't the animals that really got his attention. What he saw in front of him is what he found most intriguing. It was a forest of giant white, fluffy, seeded dandelions.

"Wimberlies," the professor stated. "They are like pine tree sized dandelions that always stay in a seeded state and never actually bloom. We should find the queen Muzz Bug in the heart of the forest."

"It could take us an hour just to get there," Charlie said.

"No worries, Charlie-dude," said Jagger, then touched the screen on a high-tech wristband he was wearing and a compartment at the base of the ship opened up. Two jet powered flying motorbikes were exposed. "You reckon' you can handle one of those bad boys?" Jagger asked Charlie.

Charlie, almost salivating, replied, "I think you'd be surprised." The two of them retrieved the bikes and brought them to the edge of the forest.

"Addy, why don't you ride with Charlie and I can take the professor," Jagger recommended. Dr. Fox climbed on the back of Charlie's bike with no wheels and tightly gripped onto his waist.

"No bike required for me, ol' boy," said Professor Hootie and he began to flap his wings and lift off the ground.

"But, doc," Charlie began, "won't it be quicker if you just..."

The professor interrupted, "Just try and keep up." And he took off flying low but fast below the tall balls of fuzz which created a complete canopy over the forest. Just before he sped after him, Charlie glanced back at the ship and saw the ramp raising and Marvin dancing up it as it lifted. He could hear a faint, "Nnt nnt nnt nnt." He then turned with Addison clutching tightly and sped after the others.

Once speeding through the forest, Charlie really had to concentrate on what was in front of him, because what was around him was so remarkable itself. The wimberlies had slick silver stalks with no branches, nothing until the big fuzzy white puff ball of fairy-like seedlings at the top. The seedlings fell from the trees constantly which created a gentle floating snow like atmosphere. The ground was covered in the pure white seedlings, which as the bikes sped over them about two feet off the ground, left a smoke-like wake behind them. The professor was soaring low, and the two bikes swerved in and out of the silver stalks through the fairy snow. They were probably two miles in, when Charlie spotted his first Muzz

Bug. It caused him to jerk the bike slightly, startling Dr. Fox.

"Sorry," said Charlie.

"It's all right," Addison replied, understanding the circumstances.

They rode for about eight more miles into the forest with the concentration of Muzz Bugs getting denser as they rode. Some of the large, blue ladybug-like creatures were almost hovering in the air as their wings fluttered so fast you could barely see them. Some crawled across the ground and others clung to the silvery stalks of the wimberlies, but all of their colors shone much more clearly and brightly, against the sea of white seedlings, than Charlie had remembered from the one he'd seen on Earth. Whether it was the color contrast or the information the professor had shared about the Muzz Bugs, Charlie felt they were more beautiful than he had originally thought.

Professor Hootie who had been leading the way began to slow down a bit and Charlie pulled up beside him and said, "So how do we know which one is the queen? There must be thousands of Muzz Bugs in this forest."

"When we see her," the professor started, ".... we'll know."

Soon he raised his right wing indicating for the group to stop, and as the bikes idled, he lowered to where his feet touched the ground. "This is it," he said, "This is the heart of the forest. Look at that wimberly." He pointed to the stalk of a tree ahead of them. It was larger in diameter than all the rest and had markings on it. The markings Charlie recognized. It was the same yellow, zig-zag, chevron pattern that all the Muzz Bugs had on their backs. The same one that the Muzz Bug that stung his sister had. Jagger, Charlie, and Addison dismounted their bikes and walked with the professor toward the massive stalk. A multitude of Muzz Bugs began to surround them as the outsiders moved closer to where a pile of Muzz Bugs were gathered at the base of the fat, marked wimberly. Charlie could tell that Jagger was getting nervous, and he realized that the professor had never really educated Jagger on the Muzz Bug. All Jagger knew was that Lizzie had been stung by one of these creatures and was now paralyzed as a result. Jagger's mind had to be thinking "if a sting from one can paralyze what would a couple hundred do." Jagger kept his right hand as close to his right boot as he could while they walked. Charlie wondered what he had in that boot. It was at that moment the professor spoke up, "We are here to see the Queen," he announced.

Right then, the wind picked up and the silver stalks began to bend and seedlings began to fall like a blizzard had arrived. Charlie was now getting a bit nervous himself. The pile of Muzz Bugs began to move like water, rising on the sides creating a bowl and rim, then pushing in toward the middle. The center raised out of the bowl and right on the very peak of the hundred or so Muzz Bugs, working together in unison, was a Muzz Bug unlike all the rest. She was double in size and where the other bugs had shiny, navy blue wings with the yellow chevron pattern, hers sparkled, like she was covered in navy and gold glitter. And as she turned around toward the intruders, Charlie could detect what appeared to be a tiny diamond crown on her small black head.

"I'm going with...that's the queen," Charlie said lowly.

"I told you you'd know," Professor Hootie responded never taking his eyes off the queen.

The Queen then spoke, "And for what reason do we have guests in our forest?"

"You're highness," began the professor, "we are on a most honorable quest."

"I'll be the judge of that!" the Queen snapped back.

"Yes, of course, your highness. Well you see, as far fetched as it may seem, it appears a Muzz Bug found it's way to Earth over in Galaxy 5..."

"I know where Earth is," the Queen interrupted. "What do you take me for, a fool?"

"No, no, of course not your highness. Anyway this boy's sister was..."

"My sister was stung by a the Muzz Bug. The Muzz Bug that came to Earth," Charlie blurted out.

"You mean she was 'transfused'," the Queen corrected him.

"Look, call it what you want, but my little sister is out there paralyzed and if we don't help her she's going to die. Now I've heard the legend of the anti-venom and the professor here has also educated me on your culture, which I must say I admire tremendously. We humans can't sacrifice ourselves to save a loved one like you guys can... God knows I would if I could... this legend of the anti-venom is all the hope I have. So, will you please help us ma'am? Will you please help my little sister, Lizzie?"

"Lizzie? Well that's *my* name," the Queen responded with a completely changed tone to her voice. "My boy, you seem as honorable as a Muzz Bug, and it would give me great pleasure to share with you this piece of information, that has been passed down to me by my ancestors. Why, I would be the first queen in ten generations to share it with someone."

"So it's true?!" Charlie exclaimed, "The Legend is true?"

"Oh yes, my boy, the legend is very much true. You just have to promise one thing."

"Sure. What is it?"

"If and when you find this 'anti-venom', you can tell no one of it's location, for it could mean the end of our species," Queen Lizzie warned.

"Of course," Charlie said. "We all completely agree to that. Right guys?"

The other three nodded and said, "Yes. We promise."

"Very well then," the Queen continued, "I'm sure you are eager because I know time is of the essence, so I'll get right to it. The words that have been given to me are these: **In the depths, you'll find an idol, with ten limbs, but no legs**."

Jagger typed the clue they'd just been given into the screen of his wristband. The other's were just repeating it over in their heads.

The Queen spoke again, "Now I've been holding those words for sixty years and I've got a pretty good idea what they mean, but as the tradition would have it I'm not allowed to express any of my own thoughts toward this."

Charlie looked at the professor, who said with confidence, "I'm pretty sure I know where we're going next."

Charlie turned back to Queen Lizzie, and said, "Thank you ma'am. You have done your part, and for that I am grateful. It was an honor to meet you and to visit your home."

The group mounted their bikes and prepared to head back to the ship, when the Queen called out, "It was Clyde."

Confused, Charlie asked, "What was?"

"The Muzz Bug who went to Earth. He disappeared last year. He was just sixteen years old himself, but two of my faithful said they saw him sneak onto a research ship. He always was a curious one, that Clyde. Anyway, sorry about your sister, Lizzie. I wish you the best of luck on you quest."

And with that, they sped away again into the "snowy" forest. As he rode, Charlie began thinking about Clyde the Muzz Bug, who he'd kicked and hated. He now realized Clyde was just a scared teenager, four galaxies away from home, trying to find something that could give himself comfort. Charlie now realized why the young Muzz Bug was lying in that patch of dandelions in the woods behind his house-- poor Clyde must have been homesick.

CHAPTER 7

DECIPHERING THE QUEEN'S CLUE

(56 HOURS LEFT)

The group returned to the ship as quickly as possible and having received Jagger's call ahead, Marvin had the ramp and the bike bay open for them. Charlie was dying to pick the professor's brain about the clue Queen Lizzie had given them, but he saw no need to do so until they got back to the ship. The bikes were parked and the crew began to board Lady Alabama once more.

As they entered, Jagger beat Charlie to the punch, "So doc, where we headed next?"

"Semtara," announced the professor with confidence.

77

"How can you be so sure?" asked Charlie.

"Well, the Queen's clue started 'In the depths', and Semtara is a planet made of water with a solid core located deep within the water."

Dr. Fox chimed in, "Yes but couldn't it mean one of the 'cave planets'? They also have very deep caverns and crevices if I recall from Geography 101."

"Right you are, Addison," Professor Hootie said proudly, "and I too thought of this, but the end of the clue indicates..."

"Some sort of tree," Jagger interrupted, feeling pretty proud of himself.

"I don't believe so," the professor continued. "I believe the 'limbs' are referring to arms and legs, not the branches of a tree."

Charlie spoke up, "But the clue said 'no legs', and what kind of creature has ten arms."

"I can think of plenty," stated Dr. Fox, remembering some of her alien anatomy courses from med school.

"Yes, but not in this planetary system," said Dr. Hootie.

"So it's a tree then, doc," Jagger insisted.

"No. There is a sea creature found on Semtara that can also be found on Earth. In fact, there are some who believe that the creatures found on Earth actually were brought there from Semtara... but that's a whole other story." The rest of the crew waited with anticipation. "It is..... the Colossal Squid," the professor revealed.

"But professor," Charlie said, "don't squids just have eight arms? The clue said ten arms."

"Ahh," said the professor, "the clue said 'ten limbs' and yes, they have eight arms, but..."

"But they also have two tentacles," finished Addison, "which are also considered limbs."

The professor smiled, "Correct. In fact, the Colossal Squid uses these tentacles to actually grab food and bring it in to eat almost like arms. And, I happen to know that there is a forty foot tall golden Colossal Squid statue in the middle of Semtara's capital city, Mantle."

"An 'idol'," whispered Charlie.

"Yeah, definitely not a tree," Jagger said and Marvin shook his head in agreement with his captain. "Sounds like the professor's got it! So let's get moving."

Marvin's bass tones started up as he and Jagger went to work at their control panels, and within minutes the spaceship was back in outer space headed now toward the water planet, Semtara.

Chapter 8

Semtara

(54 hours left)

It took them about 2 hours to travel to Semtara, with Charlie constantly glancing at his watch to keep an eye on the countdown. He had asked Jagger why they couldn't go as fast as they did before when traveling across galaxies, and Jagger explained to him that if he turned back on the ultra-light speed hyper-drive that they'd fly clear past Semtara and into the next galaxy. So, Charlie just ate some Cheetos and beef jerky and rode as patiently as possible.

Once into view, Charlie could see the strange planet. He had pictured it being blue like the way water looked on Earth from space, but this water was clear like a bubble or a snow globe with a center core that you could see from the surface which appeared to be golden.

"It's clear," stated Charlie.

"Crystal clear," responded Professor Hootie. "Otherwise no light would get to the surface."

"How deep is it?" asked Addison.

"It's a good eight kilometers, " said the professor.

Charlie quickly did the math conversions in his head, and exclaimed, "That's over 26,000 feet!"

The professor grinned and said,"...'In the depths'." He then got a kind of startled look on his face and turned to Jagger. "Where will you land? And how will we get to the surface?" Charlie could tell this was the first time the professor had thought of this dilemma, and because it concerned him so, it also concerned Charlie.

But Jagger quickly responded seeing the worried looks he was getting, "It's cool. It's cool. I told y'all Lady Alabama isn't just your ordinary, run-of-the-mill space ship. She's also a fully functional submarine.... when I want her to be. Comes in handy sometimes even on Earth-- the Atlantic Ocean can be a pretty good hiding place..." Jagger kind of stopped himself like he was maybe saying too much that he shouldn't, then started back, "She may lose a little speed in the water, but another fifteen to twenty minutes and we'll be to the core." Charlie and the others breathed a sigh of relief.

As they got closer to the planet, Charlie saw little dots moving throughout the water. At this range, the planet reminded Charlie of slides he'd looked at under a microscope in science class with little microorganisms swimming around. He soon realized these were sea creatures of all sorts swimming around their planet. Then they reached the surface of the water, and Jagger slowed the ship to almost a stop. "No need to make a big splash. Don't think the locals would take too kindly to it," he said, and the nose of Lady Alabama entered first, then the windshield became completely submerged, and right as the back end of the ship was about go into the water Jagger yelled back at Marvin, "Submarine mode...NOW!"

Charlie looked back at Marvin and saw him touch a screen then pinch his nose-like bump with his left hand and with his right hand turned to the side and raised above his head, brought it down in front of his pinched nose with a squiggly water motion. Immediately, there was a thud and the sound of some hydraulics, then like fans were turned on, and Jagger once again said, "Giddy-up!" He pushed his controls forward and the ship went speeding smoothly through the water, leaving virtually no wake behind them. As they did, they first passed a school of fish that were bright pink, green, and purple with bugle-like noses and long feather-like tails. They saw yellow jellyfish-like creatures, large turquoise and silver rays, a multitude of other colorful fish groups, and even passed an orange colossal squid that must have been fifteen feet long. To Charlie's amazement, it really never got darker the further down they went.

As they neared the core, it now became clear that the gold color seen from space was from a golden latticed dome, that encompassed the core, which created a fenced barrier between the core's land and inhabitants and that of the water above. Before they could actually get all the way to the golden dome, the ship was met by about fifty beings riding a mixture of giant seahorses and weedy sea dragons that were all bright, multicolored, beautiful creatures. The beings riding them looked like men with flesh colored skin from their waists up. They were all lean and muscular and had gills in the area of their ribs. Their legs were covered in silver and gold reflective scales with golden webbed feet, and they were all holding what appeared to be harpoon guns.

Jagger, who was once again a bit nervous, said, "Hey doc, should we be worried about this?"

The professor responded, "Just let me do the talking," and he moved up to where Jagger was sitting.

At that time the Semtarian in the front said, "Goob goob glob blob?" Jagger took off his wristband, touched a few buttons, handed it to Professor Hootie, and said, "Be my guest."

The professor held the wristband close to his mouth and spoke into it, "Blib blob gool goo glob glob glee." He turned to the rest of the crew and said, "Semtara is one of the planets that has refused to adopt English as it's official language."

"So what did he say," asked Dr. Fox.

"He asked why they should allow us entry?"

"And what did you tell them?" asked Charlie.

"I told them we have heard of their great golden statue and wanted to see it for ourselves."

"Gloop bloop ool gloop blob blob glee?" asked the merman after some deliberation with one his companions.

"He says 'he can assure us it is great indeed'," translated Dr. Hootie, then replied, "Plip plop gloop glop glum glum glee. Bloop plop glip glop blip bloop gloo." He turned back to the crew and said, "I have told him we are judges in a contest to see which planet's statue is most impressive, and we need to examine their Golden Colossal Squid to see how it compares with the Great Lunar Moth statue on the planet Actias."

"And you think that will work?" Charlie asked with an unconvinced voice.

The head Semtarian guardsman motioned for the ship to follow them and said,"Blib blub bloo."

The professor looked at Charlie and said, "It appears it did."

Jagger followed the convoy of guardsmen to a spot on the dome where three of the men climbed off their large sea horses and onto the dome. They each removed necklaces which had keys at the end, and they simultaneously placed the keys into locks on the latticed dome. The three of them then reached down and pulled open a gate which was not big enough for the ship to fit through.

"Well," said Jagger, "looks like this is as far as she goes," and he parked Lady Alabama on top of the dome. He then said, "I have only two dive suits on this ship, so that means not everybody is getting to go the rest of the way."

"I'm really not a very good swimmer," stated the professor.

"Good," replied Jagger, " 'cause I don't think you and your tall self would have fit in one anyway."

"Well I'm going," stated Charlie quickly.

"I would like to, as well," said Dr. Fox, "but if you want the other suit Jagger, I mean, I understand."

"Well ain't you in luck, Addy," said Jagger, "cause this fella here does want to go, but I don't need a suit. I'm good underwater for a couple of hours, and I really don't plan on us being down there that long."

As Charlie and Addison suited up and Jagger changed from his flight suit to a wet suit, which showed off his fit physique even better, Professor Hootie communicated with the guardsman that the three crew members were going to swim down to evaluate the statue closely, and they would be taking some pictures of the details on the squid which would be used to make the "judges final decision".

Marvin started up a beat, and using his control panel, a door in the floor of the ship opened which contained a small compartment, an airlock, that the three divers climbed down into.

"Remember," said the professor, "take pictures of everything. You never know what might be important, and this is probably our only chance to look at this thing." With that, Marvin closed the door in the floor over their heads. A moment later another door below them opened and Charlie, Addison, and Jagger found themselves in the water with the Semtarian guardsmen. The leader motioned for three of the men to escort the visitors down, and the six of them swam through the large golden gate toward the surface.

As they approached the capital city from overhead, Charlie marveled at the beauty of the city. All the buildings were made of silver and trimmed in gold. There were lots of people moving about. Some were swimming, some were riding on seahorses, weedy sea dragons, or other large colorful fish, and some were actually walking with weighted shoes on. He saw a silver statue in a park of an eight feet wide clam with a pearl the size of a basketball in it. There were kids playing, chasing each other through hoops and around coral. Then they approached the capital building which was magnificent in itself, but was quickly overshadowed by the enormous golden statue which stood in its courtyard. One of he escorts turned to the three of them and actually speaking English simply said, "One hour." They could tell he meant what he said, so with each of them equipped with a camera, they began taking pictures like crazy, not even really sure what they were looking for. After about thirty minutes of this, Addison stopped and just began swimming around examining the creature.

"What are you doing, Addy?" asked Jagger. "You heard what the doc said. We need to photograph everything."

"I was just thinking about the clue," she said. "Just trying to work smarter, not harder. I just feel like maybe we should be focusing more on the limbs."

"I've gotten plenty of pictures of the limbs," said Jagger, but as he was talking Charlie began to think Dr. Fox was right. He swam up to one of the tentacles and began to examine it very closely. On the underside of it, about half way down he noticed something etched in the gold. He ran his fingers over it, then shouted, "I found a number!"

The other two, quickly swam over to him and looked, "It's a nine," said Charlie.

"Or is it a six," Addison responded. They snapped a picture of the number and then, each of them moved to a different limb.

Jagger spoke up next from one of the arms, "This one says 'SOUTH'!" and he clicked his camera.

"I found the word 'THE' on this arm," exclaimed Dr. Fox, while Charlie had moved to the other tentacle and anounced, "This one has the letter 'J'."

They methodically moved to each of the remaining arms and took pictures of all the etchings.

When the hour was up the three Semtarian guardsmen returned, ready to use force if necessary to get the "judges" to leave. But as they arrived at the statue, they found that the visitors had already swum away.

About ten minutes earlier, Charlie, Addison, and Jagger had swum through the gate in the dome, and were back in the airlock at the bottom of Lady Alabama. Jagger gave three hard knocks against the door above them, which initiated the doors below them to close, the water quickly drained from the small room, and in sequence the doors above them opened once more.

Chapter 9

Deciphering the Squid's Clue

(51 hours left)

Back in the ship, all the photos were uploaded to the ship's main computer, and were put in a sphere in the middle of the ship. The crew gazed at the sphere and examined the photos for a few minutes, then Addison asked Marvin, "Can we just see the photos of the words?"

Quickly, only ten photos were present, and the sphere had become a flat surface where the words could all be seen together. They read: SOUTH, ON, POLE, WHERE, FLAG, THE, 6, COLD, IT'S, J.

"Were they in any particular order," asked Professor Hootie.

Charlie replied, " Maybe, but we were moving so fast, we didn't really pay attention. I do know that the 6, or 9, and the J were on the tentacles, and the words were on the arms."

"I feel like the words create a sentence," said the professor contemplating the words before him, "but I'm not sure about the J and the 6, or 9."

Dr. Fox began shifting the images of the words around. First she moved the 6/9 and the J to the side, then shifted the words to say IT'S THE COLD POLE WHERE ON SOUTH FLAG. Everyone shook their head and she shifted them again to say ON THE FLAG POLE WHERE IT'S COLD SOUTH.

"Still doesn't seem right," said Charlie. "Can I try?" He began to shift the words himself. THE FLAG POLE ON THE SOUTH WHERE IT'S COLD.

The crew thought about this for a few seconds, then Professor Hootie said, "I think you're close, but lets try this." He changed a few words to create the sentence FLAG ON THE SOUTH POLE WHERE IT'S COLD. Each crew member read the sentence to themselves and agreed that the sentence made sense, but then Charlie asked, "But what does it mean? Every planet in this system has north and south poles. Is there just one that is cold?"

"On the contrary, my boy," began the professor, "I would say the majority of the south poles in this system are cold."

Charlie looked discouraged, and Addison turned to Jagger and said, "Could 6 J be coordinates?"

"It'd be J 6, but you need more than just the one coordinate to find anything," replied Jagger.

The professor quickly looked up at Jagger and said, "What did you just say? Say that again."

Jagger looked confused and hesitantly said, "You need more than just one coordinate to find anything?"

"No, not that. Before, you said," and the professor shifted the 6 and J to make J and 6, "You said 'J 6'. Marvin, can you pull back up the map of Galaxy 9, System 7."

Marvin instantly did and the professor pointed, "There," he said pointing to a planet with a dark black ring bisecting the planet, "This is the planet, Jaysics. It is a completely uninhabited planet whose northern hemisphere is a hot dry desert with rivers of lava, and whose southern hemisphere is a frozen tundra of snow caps and glaciers."

"Sounds like we've got a destination, Doc," stated Jagger as he moved into his pilot seat.

"So, professor, you said it was uninhabited, but is there a flag on the south pole?" asked Charlie.

"I guess we'll just have to see, won't we," said the bird-man with a grin. Marvin's beat box sounds started up and the ship began moving to the surface of Semtara. It burst out of the water and back into space, and began its journey toward the south pole of Jaysics.

CHAPTER 10

THE COLD SIDE OF JAYSICS

(47 HOURS LEFT)

Approximately four hours after emerging from the clear waters of Semtara, the Lady Alabama was approaching the south pole of Jaysics. Charlie marveled at how distinctly different the two sides of the planet were. From a distance the planet was cut in half; the top half being orange with hot dry sand and rivers of lava, and the bottom half completely white with snow. As the ship began to get into position to enter the planet's atmosphere at the south pole, Charlie heard Jagger say, "Whoa," and then "Hey doc, we may have an issue here."

"I see it," Professor Hootie replied as he stared out the front of the ship. Charlie, Dr. Fox, and Marvin all brought their focus to the view in front of them. It was a swirling group of clouds which looked gray against the white contrast of all the snow.

"*It's* right where *we* need to be," stated Jagger. "We might need to hold back and wait for this storm to pass."

"Wait?" asked Charlie, once again looking at his watch which read **46:51:50**. "We can't wait. We don't have time to wait."

Jagger looked at the professor as if to say "Back me up here", but he got a different answer.

"The boy is right, Captain. Storms in the southern hemisphere can stay in the same place for weeks. We can't take that chance." He paused, then asked, "You ever flown a ship in a blizzard?"

"A time or two," responded Jagger.

"Well, this isn't a blizzard, it's what is called a blizzarcane," informed the professor. Charlie and Dr. Fox looked at each other and repeated, "blizzarcane" in concerned voices. "Yes. Jaysics is said to have some of the most magnificent ones in the universe."

"Yeah, pretty certain I've never flown in one of those," said Jagger. Then he turned and shouted to Marvin, "Stay with me here, buddy. I'm gonna need ya." And Jagger put a head set microphone on and Marvin followed suit. "It looks like the eye is directly over the south pole, so, that's where we're going in. Marvin, be ready with the wind resisters and the throttle adjusters. We're going straight down the eye and we're gonna be spinning as we go. Hold on everybody," and the crew, already secured by the ship's energy seat belts, braced themselves.

The ship tipped its nose down and after a deep breath, Jagger pushed the throttle and the ship sped downward toward the eye of the blizzarcane. As it entered the ship began to spin in the same direction the storm seemed to be moving. Charlie was kind of surprised at how smooth everything seemed to be going. But soon they began to get close to the surface and had to slow down. Then the ship had to turn from its vertical inclination to once again being horizontally oriented. As it did so, a gust of wind grabbed the ship and threw it. The ship tumbled through wind and snow for probably five miles.

"Wind resisters, Marvin!" Jagger yelled, "Wind resisters!" Marvin quickly responded, and the ship seemed to gain back a slight bit of control. "We've got to fight through this, Marvin. That gust threw us the wrong way. We've got to get back to where we were and go a little further east. Turn on the throttle adjusters and set them to 350." Marvin followed his captains orders. "Alright, lower the resisters." As Marvin did so, Jagger began pushing the ship back toward the eye, into a head wind that must have been 200mph. Charlie could feel the resistance on the ship as they flew slowly back the direction they had come. Snow and ice like he'd never seen before pelted the ship constantly.

The ship made it back to the eye of the storm, and things calmed a bit. Charlie asked, "Anybody see a flagpole?"

Jagger replied as if he'd forgotten why they were even there, "Flagpole? I don't know how we're going to see anything in this."

"We'll keep our eyes open," said Addison to give some comfort to Charlie.

After another deep breath, Jagger again pushed forward flying east and leaving the calm-ish eye of the blizzarcane. The snow and ice once again banged into the ship loudly and the ship seemed to be flying blind through the density of the storm. Charlie squinted as he peered out the front of the Lady Alabama, when all of a sudden he saw something. It was just a speck, but it was something.

"There!" he shouted. "Do you see that?"

The rest of the crew looked, but didn't see anything. Charlie said, "I swear it, there was something there. It was glowing orange."

"Did it look like a flag?" asked Jagger.

"Well, I couldn't tell. Not really, but it was something. Go toward the left a little," Charlie requested. Jagger was about to tell him that wasn't the proper course, but as he double checked it, he realized that they had once agin been blown slightly off track and Charlie was correct in where they should be headed.

As he turned and they proceeded forward, Addison shouted, "There it is! I see it, too!"

They moved toward the glowing orange object which looked more like a torch than a flag. When they got close enough, they realized why. The wind had wrapped the flag around the top of the pole. "Wind resistors up!" ordered Jagger again. Marvin did so and the ship stabilized a bit. "So now what?" Jagger said

"We have to get the flag to get the clue," exclaimed Charlie.

"We can't take the flag," replied Dr. Fox, "We have to leave all the clues in tact for future incidents."

Charlie knew she was right, so he revised his statement, "We need to unwrap the flag and get the clue."

"And how do you propose we do that?" asked Jagger. "I'm not sure how long I'll be able to hold Lady here."

"I'll do it," stated Professor Hootie. The crew turned toward him, confused.

"Do what?" said Addison.

"I'll go out there and untangle the flag. One of you can get a picture of it through the windshield," commanded the professor.

"Professor, it's way too dangerous!" said Addison.

"It has to be done and I'm the best equipped for the job. Do any of the rest of you have talons that can grip onto tree branches, or flagpoles? Do any of the rest of you have a natural coating on you that helps you to be wind and water resistant?" The crew began to realize he was right and that there was no talking him out of it. "Jagger can you get the ship right over the flagpole?"

"I think so, Doc, but holding her there is another story."

"Just do the best you can. I've got faith in you."

Jagger and Marvin repositioned the ship slowly with the wind resisters up. Professor Hootie climbed into the airlock in the floor. With the ship positioned directly over the flag pole, the floor closed over Professor Hootie's head and within seconds his floor opened below him and he dropped from the ship. Almost instantaneously, a gust of wind caught the ship and sent it sailing back, tumbling about a mile from the pole. The crew initially wanted to panic, but quickly realized it would do no good. Once Jagger and Marvin had the ship stabilized and headed back in the right direction, Charlie glanced back to where Lizzie was lying, still safely on her energy bed, as if the ship had never moved. The main focus was quickly turned toward finding the professor. They weren't even sure if he'd made it to the pole, and if he had, how long could he stay out in these conditions.

As they once again, slowly flew against the strong winds and snow, Addison piped up, "Look!" she exclaimed, "The flag!" They all looked ahead and it was immediately apparent that the flag was different than before. It no longer looked like a torch, but an actual flag from the distance. A glowing orange rectangular flag. As they got closer, they saw an image attached to the flag. It was the professor.

Professor Hootie had his hands clutching the end of the flag. He was completely horizontal, blowing in the wind like he was part of the flag, but by doing so he kept the flag open and still enough for Charlie to quickly pull out his camera and snapped a picture of the flag, not even taking time to the read the words printed on it. "Got it," he said.

"How are we going to get him back in?" asked Dr. Fox to Jagger. They could see ice and snow sticking to the professor's feathers, eyes, and hands and knew he couldn't hold on much longer.

Jagger contemplated a few seconds only, then said, "Marvin, get the chute ready. I have an idea." He maneuvered the ship so that its back end was close to the flag pole. He announced over a microphone to the outside of the ship, "Doc, you have to trust me here. When I count to three, you have to let go of the flag." He turned to Marvin, "Marvin, release the chute just before I say three. Got it?" Marvin gave a thumbs up from his co-pilot chair. Jagger once again into the microphone, "Ok, doc, here we go....1...2...3."

Everything happened at once. Marvin released a chute from the back of the ship like a car at the end of a drag race, which of course was caught by the blizzarcane's winds and once again sent the ship sailing back toward the eye of the storm. Jagger immediately yelled, "Reel it in! Reel in the chute!" Had the professor done his part and let go? No one knew yet. By the time the ship hit the eye, the chute had been completely reeled into the back of the ship and the captain was able to once again gain control of the Lady Alabama. Jagger quickly turned the ship upward and flew straight up the eye until they were above the storm.

Once they were in the calm atmosphere above the blizzarcane, the crew immediately released their energy seat belts and rushed to the rear of the ship. Marvin opened the door which led to the bay where the chute was housed. Most of the chute was wound around a wench-like apparatus, but the very tip was hanging loosely to the floor. There was a flopping around in the tip like a fish caught in a net. Then it stopped, and they heard the professor's voice say, "I hear you out there. Are you going to get me out of this blasted thing, or what?" They all burst into relieved laughter and Marvin, Charlie, and Jagger ran to manually uncrank the wench, as Dr. Fox waded through the chute trying to find an opening to get her friend out. Professor Hootie's head finally popped through an opening in the chute and the first thing he said was, "I know where we're going next!"

CHAPTER 11

THE CLUE FROM THE FLAG AND
SHIP PROBLEMS

(44 HOURS LEFT)

As the crew made its way back to the main cabin of the ship, Charlie asked, "So, you read the clue?"

"Well of course I did. What else was I going to do hanging there like a piece of laundry, not knowing when you all were coming back?" retorted Dr. Hootie. "Besides, I was afraid you all would get so caught up in rescuing me you may forget to get a picture, even though I stretched it out so nicely for you."

"Indeed you did," said Charlie as he pulled out his camera and read the clue off the picture he had taken, "**Where knights rule, and reptiles fly, Seek the weapon of the venerable guy.**"

As he finished, Professor Hootie announced, "We're going to Trikre." Jagger and Dr. Fox at the same time muttered, "Dragons." Marvin threw both his hands against the side of his face as if to say "Oh no."

Charlie checked his watch once more, which read **43:48:19**. He looked up at Jagger and said, "Well let's do it. Let's get this ship headed toward Trikre."

Jagger, understanding the urgency, replied, "You got it, boss." He turned and quickly got to his seat and started to rev the engine when "BOOM", a small explosion occurred, shaking the ship and everyone on it.

"What was that?" asked Charlie.

"I don't know," replied Jagger. "Lady got beat up pretty bad by that storm. Could be anything. Marvin, run diagnostics to see what's down."

Marvin was already running diagnostics and almost immediately turned his screen toward Jagger and pointed.

"It's our left cruiser thruster. Must have gotten too much snow and ice up in her," stated Jagger.

"How important is that?" Charlie asked in a panic. "Can it be fixed?"

Jagger replied calmly, "Pretty important, and Marvin can fix anything. It just might take a little time. But, we aren't going anywhere until its fixed."

Charlie glanced over at Lizzie peacefully sleeping. "How much time?" he asked in Marvin's direction. The purple man held up six fingers indicating six hours, which he could tell disappointed Charlie, so he quickly changed it to four fingers. Charlie nodded and Marvin jumped down from his chair and he and Jagger left the main cabin to go work on the thruster.

Charlie then turned toward the two doctors and said, "So dragons. For real?"

"Yep," they both replied.

"So, tell me about this planet: these dragons, these knights, this 'venerable' guy and his weapon," Charlie requested.

"Well," the professor began, "A few millennia ago, Trikre was a planet overrun with dangerous, deadly dragons. The other dominant species on the planet were the Wermuths, which are a small, yellow race of beings similar to humans. They are only about four and a half feet tall, but all have a warrior mentality."

"Classic Napolean complex," joked Charlie.

"Exactly," said Dr. Fox with a grin.

"Well," continued Professor Hootie, "At this time in the life of the planet, the Wermuths were living under ground, hiding from the dragons in order to survive. But then came along one Wermuth who was extremely brave and bright, and he united the others. He developed the armor that they still wear to this day, and he invented weapons which they used to fight the dragons. The first of these weapons was his, the Legendary Dragon Harpoon of Sir Grottus of Trikre. Sir Grottus was the original knight on the planet. It was under his leadership that the Wermuths took to the higher grounds and defeated the dragons."

"But, I thought you said there were still dragons?" stated Charlie.

"Oh, but there are. Not as many as there once were, but now the Wermuths control the dragons. They broke them, tamed them like wild horses. It is said that some Wermuths even ride them," Professor Hootie responded.

"So the harpoon," said Charlie," you think this is where the next clue is?"

"I feel quite certain," said the professor, "but it might not be easy to get to. The Wermuths are not known to be as welcoming as the Semtarians. And the Legendary Dragon Harpoon rests over the current ruler's chair in the great dining hall of Castle Grottus."

"Well," Addison chimed in, "looks like we'll need to get ourselves invited to dinner."

CHAPTER 12

TRIKRE AND THE WERMUTHS

(37 HOURS LEFT)

Just as Marvin had indicated, he and Jagger got Lady Alabama back in flying condition in almost exactly four hours time. It took another three to get to Trikre. During this time the team devised a plan, similar to the one they had used on Semtara, for getting into the castle and getting a look at the Legendary Dragon Harpoon of Sir Grottus. Professor Hootie explained that like the Sematarians, the Wermuth's were also very proud people.

As they entered the planet's atmosphere, Jagger spoke, "Well gang, I hope this works." The ship lowered into a field of light green grass that was waste high. The field was surrounded by weeping willows on one side and rolling hills on the other, so it was pretty well hidden. Charlie thought the planet looked very Earth-like except for the pink skies.

Dr. Fox, Professor Hootie, Jagger, and Charlie once again left the ship and retrieved the flying motorbikes from their bays. As they began to mount them, Professor Hootie said, "I think I may ride, too, this time. I wouldn't want to be mistaken for a small wild dragon." He climbed on the back of Jagger's bike and Addison on the back of Charlie's. The professor pointed and said, "Castle Grottus should be about five miles that way. It is surrounded by a mote of critch infested waters."

"Critch?" asked Charlie.

"Very much like piranha… but with more teeth," he replied.

"Sounds like a nice place to vacation," Jagger said sarcastically.

The professor reminded them as they began to head toward the castle, "Remember, let me do the talking. The Wermuth language is quite confusing in that it all sounds like normal English words, but they all mean something different. I just hope I can keep it all straight myself. One slip up and these ornery little knights could be at our throats."

"Yeah, doc, let's try to not let that happen. This turtle isn't wanting to be critch food today."

They had ridden about three miles when they spotted two dragons in the sky which were getting lower and closer. Jagger and Charlie slowed the bikes a bit. The two dragons were being ridden by little men in armor. Charlie could see the yellow tint of their skin just barely around their eyes through their helmets. The dragons flew in next to the bikes and one of the Wermuths said sternly, "Jazz!"

Professor Hootie yelled to Jagger and Charlie, "They want us to stop." The two quickly slowed their bikes to an idling hover. The two Wermuth greeters flew the dragons to position themselves face to face with the foreigners.

One of the yellow men said, "Bubbles long wash puma?"

"He's asking what we are doing here," translated the professor. Then he replied, "Pumpkin shamrock fall cougar donkey moo ham. Lavender cookie clay jump croquet. Puffy tuba pop bugle doughnut." He then whispered to the gang, "Our plan is starting. I told them we were intergalactic food critics and we were judging a soup contest, and that the famous Castle Grottus soup had been entered into the contest." As the professor explained on the flight over, the Wermuths were prideful people, and if there was anything that could rival their pride of fighting and dragon taming, it was their soups. And the most heralded soup on the planet was the one made inside Castle Grottus, simply known as Castle Grottus soup, which was rumored to contain dragon meat from the alpha dragon which Sir Grottus killed those many years ago. Legend says the Wermuths built a huge salt cellar where they have stored the body ever since.

The two Wermuths consulted one another in whispers, then turned and spoke once again. "Planktan larva mohawk goat. Llama coffee shire smell." The professor translated, "They say they don't need foreigners to tell them their soup is the best, but they are okay with us telling the rest of the universe." Then the two dragons turned around, and one flew to the back of the hover bikes, as to keep an eye on the aliens, while the Wermuth on the dragon still in front of them motioned and yelled, "Salami!", and the convoy began toward the castle.

As they arrived to the mote, they were met by four more Wermuth guards on dragons. After a quick update by the first two Wermuths, they were escorted over the mote to the castle. As they flew over the black waters of the mote, Charlie couldn't help but look down, and it appeared the water was bubbling. "It's the critch," Dr. Fox said seeing the puzzled look on Charlie's face. "There must be thousands of them."

As they arrived at the castle, they parked their bikes, next to a rail, where the Wermuths parked their dragons, tied to a post like horses in a western movie. The crew was then escorted into Castle Grottus by a dozen Wermuths. Off the dragons, and now standing next to them, Charlie didn't think the Wermuths seemed quite as scary. He was about a foot and a half taller than everyone of them, but he didn't love the way they kept spears pointed at him and the others at all times. The castle was grand and made out of stone. It had tall arch ways and long corridors and reminded Charlie of castles he'd seen in movies and pictures on Earth. In every room they went through, Charlie noticed the same flag he'd seen flying outside on every corner of the castle as they had arrived. It was a yellow flag, which had three points at the unattached end. On it was a picture of a Wermuth with a spear in one hand and one foot stepping on the throat of a dragon that was lying on the ground. Charlie just assumed that particular Wermuth was Sir Grottus.

They were first led to the current ruler of Trikre, Sir Mantis, who upon hearing about these soup critics, welcomed them. They were finally led by Sir Mantis himself, to a large dining hall, which was filled with fifty, or more, Wermuths. As they entered, Sir Mantis picked up a mallet and hit a large gong, which immediately rang through the room and silenced the chattering, eating Wermuths. They all turned their attention toward the new entrants into the hall.

"Pelican!", Sir Mantis shouted.

"Listen up," the professor quietly translated to the crew.

"Tulip fairy junebug croquet grumpy salad shoe. Frugal donkey water side shimmy coy caterpillar."

"These guests are here to try our soup and tell all the galaxies it is the best."

Jagger whispered, "Check it out, Chuck," and he lifted his chin as to direct Charlie's vision to a wall across the hall. Charlie quickly spotted it; the Legendary Dragon Harpoon of Sir Grottus of Trikre. It was hanging on the wall about eighty feet away above the fanciest chair in the room. Charlie's adrenaline started rushing as he knew the next clue was so close by and his sister was back at the ship with her life dependent on saving time. He looked down at his watch which read **36:11:45**. He turned to the professor, and whispered, "I'm going for it."

The professor, showing concern, quickly replied, "Let's stick to the plan. We'll get to it in due time."

"We don't have that time to waste," said Charlie and he began quickly walking across the hall.

Professor Hootie began frantically rattling off all sorts of random words, stuttering a bit trying not to make a mistake, explaining to Sir Mantis that the young boy was a historian at heart and was interested in their great relic on the wall. By the time the professor got this out of his mouth and before any of the Wermuths could hardly move,

Charlie had jumped onto the arms of the large chair and had taken the harpoon off the wall and began to study it, oblivious to his surroundings. Then he heard a shout, "Jazzercize!" The shout came form Sir Mantis, who as Charlie turned back, appeared to be in a fit of anger.

"Run for it, Charlie!" shouted Professor Hootie as Wermuths began to jump from their seats and come after the crew members.

The professor pushed away from two Wermuths, backed out of the dining hall, and quickly flew up to the high ceilings of the castle to try to elude the little warriors. Jagger did a quick duck and roll to get away from the Wermuths holding spears and reached into his boot and pulled out a small gun from which he began shooting laser bullets. Charlie, up higher than his pursuers, with his adrenaline really flowing now, and the harpoon in his hands, began using the legendary relic as a bow staff. He was kicking, hitting, and tossing Wermuths that were coming at him in every direction. His size advantage mixed with his extraordinary skills in the martial arts mixed with his adrenaline rush, had Charlie fighting off tens of Wermuths at a time. Jagger glanced over at him in between shots and was awed by what he saw; the spinning, the kicking, the flipping..."Who is this kid?" Jagger thought, but only briefly as he once again fired a shot to fend off Wermuths coming at him.

As the two of them piled up a room full of Wermuth shrapnel, and with only a few of the little warriors remaining on their feet, they heard a scream for help, and they simultaneously realized… Addison had been captured. The only Wermuths with weapons were those who had escorted them into the dining hall, and with the other three crew members having escaped, all spears had gotten turned toward Addison. Charlie and Jagger looked at each other and then at the remaining few Wermuths who at this point realized they were no match for these two foreigners, and turned to run out of the hall. Charlie and Jagger also ran for the door to try to find Addison, and hoped Professor Hootie had gotten away.

As they left the dining hall and entered the castle corridors they had just walked through, they were struck by the eerie silence and absence of Wermuths. They began to proceed with caution, Jagger with his gun gripped close and Charlie still clutching the harpoon. They entered a large room with tall ceilings and Jagger nodded his head directing Charlie's eyes to three spears lodged into the tall ceiling of the large room.

"The Professor," whispered Jagger.

"I don't see any feathers," said Charlie, "so that's a good sign. Where do you think they're taking Dr. Fox?"

"I think if we're lucky they're locking her in a dungeon somewhere, otherwise...they're gonna make her critch food."

They wandered aimlessly through the large castle seeing no sign of Addison or any Wermuths for quite some time. As they searched, Charlie quietly asked, "So back on Earth, at the arcade, you told Dr. Fox you owed her. What did you mean by that?"

Jagger replied in a whisper, "About two years ago I was a bit strapped for cash, so Marvin and I headed over to Mars which has gotten a reputation for gambling on spaceship drag races. I may have indicated I was kind of a 'newbie' pilot, and then I kind of won a race around Jupiter and back."

"You hustled them," Charlie interrupted.

Jagger shrugged his shoulders as if to say "a man's gotta do what a man's gotta do."

"When I went to collect my winnings," Jagger continued, "a guy was there I went to flight school with, and he ratted me out. I guess it didn't go over so well because a Limrit shot me in the shoulder with a laser blaster. With a little help from Marvin, I managed to get onto the ship and out of there. We flew straight to the hospital on Earth, and Addison got me fixed up." He opened his flight suit a little to show Charlie the scar on his shoulder. "The laser had cauterized all the blood vessels going to my arm. If Addison hadn't done what she did, I would have lost it," he said patting his arm.

About that time they saw a Wermuth holding a spear run by and enter a corridor on the other side of the room. The little man had not spotted the two of them. Jagger and Charlie decided to follow him. At the end of the corridor they found a spiral staircase leading only down. From the top they heard Addison's voice yelling, "Get your hands off me you little creeps!" The two rushed down the stairs, and were immediately met by two guards, which before Jagger could blast them, Charlie did a jump spin crescent kick which caught both guards across the jaw and sent them both to the ground knocked out cold.

Charlie looked back at Jagger who had a look of impressed disbelief on his face, and Jagger said, "Okay, I know now is not the time, but at some point we're gonna have to talk about this." Charlie tried to hold it back, but a little smirk came to his face for a split second, and then the two were back completely focused on the mission. They swiftly but cautiously moved down the hall, passing some closed dungeon cells with iron bars. They would quickly glance in each to see if Dr. Fox was in them, but she was not. There was a bend to the right at the end of the hall. As they made the turn, four more guards came charging at them from forty feet away. Jagger fired his gun and one of the guards dropped, but another flung a spear which flew directly toward Jagger's face. Charlie yelled, "Duck!" and he ran in front of Jagger just as the spear arrived. He bent backward like he was going under a limbo stick, karate chopped his hand up and out, and caught the spear right in the middle, breaking it in half and throwing it off it's course. He then sprinted down the hall toward the three Wermuths, and just before he reached them he leapt to the side wall, pushing off with one leg, and again using the Legendary Harpoon of Sir Grottus as a bow staff, wielded it around with great speed striking two of the three little knights. The third had managed to avoid the attack and had raised his spear in order to counterattack. As he began to thrust the spear at Charlie, a blast from Jagger's laser pistol sent the Wermuth flying back and to the floor.

The two rounded another corner at the end of that hall, and as they looked down the length of the next corridor they were surprised to see daylight. Probably sixty yards away the corridor was open to the outside. They heard a whistle and glimpsed Sir Mantis grab Addison, whose hands were now tied. He threw her on the back of a dragon who had flown to the opening. Sir Mantis also boarded the creature and they took off. There were about ten more Wermuths at the end of the hall. One turned and spotted Charlie and Jagger and yelled, "Jazzercize!" Six of the Wermuths came at them, as two more jumped onto another dragon and flew away. Jagger fired his pistol down the hall causing one of the Wermuths to hit against the wall and then drop to the floor. Charlie turned to Jagger, handed him the harpoon and said, "Cover me. I'm going for the next dragon."

He then sprinted toward the five warriors and about ten feet before them he went into cartwheel roundoff back flip, soaring over top of the little knights catching two of them with backhand hammer fists while he was upside down above them. Jagger blasted down the hall as Charlie was in the air, clear of the path. Charlie heard another whistle as he landed to his feet on the other side of the Wermuths. He still had twenty yards to sprint as he saw a dragon pull up and the other two Wermuths begin to board. Both Wermuths mounted the beast, and as they began to fly away, Charlie, still in full sprint, leapt from the opening, soaring about eight feet in the air and landing on the back of the winged creature. Charlie quickly gathered himself and as he did he looked down and was surprised to see just how high in the air they were. He had thought since they had entered the castle on ground level and then actually gone down stairs that they would be closer to the ground, but he now realized there was a huge ravine on the back side of Castle Grottus that appeared to be a couple of hundred feet deep. He grabbed the closest Wermuth and tossed him from the dragon. The other Wermuth flew the dragon close to the ground and before Charlie could grab him, he jumped from the beast on his own and rolled across the ground.

Back at the castle, Jagger had reached the opening himself and realizing how high off the ground he was, he touched the screen on his wristband and spoke into it, "Pick me up." Within a minute, his flying motorbike had arrived at the opening and Jagger boarded the craft with his pistol now holstered and holding the Legendary

Harpoon of Sir Grottus. He swiftly took off after the dragons.

Charlie, having never driven a dragon before, was having difficulties, but he was able to keep Addison and Sir Mantis in his sights ahead and they appeared to be heading to the mote. Jagger caught up to Charlie and Charlie happily made the transition onto the back of Jagger's bike. Jagger handed him the harpoon back and said, "Here, you may need this."

They sped toward Addison and caught up to them right as Sir Mantis was trying to push her off the back of his dragon into the bubbling critch filled waters below. With her hands still tied she began to fall forward with prodding from his spear. Charlie, reaching out, was able to grab her hands, but as he did, Sir Mantis grabbed onto her feet and flew the dragon slightly away. Addison was now creating a bridge between the two flying objects, which were at least 300 feet above the mote below. Charlie knew if he let go, then so would Sir Mantis, and Dr. Fox would drop into the waters and be eaten alive. So, he did the only thing he could think of to get Sir Mantis to let go first…… he dropped the Legendary Dragon Harpoon of Sir Grottus.

Sir Mantis, seeing the worshiped relic falling toward the saw-like jaws of the critch, immediately releases Dr. Fox and quickly steered his dragon down toward the falling object. Addison's legs dropped and her weight shift jerked the motorbike down causing Charlie to lose his balance. He over compensated by pulling back, thrusting Addison up onto the bike, but when he did, he could not regain his own balance and fell backwards off the bike. Like the harpoon, he too was now plunging toward the bubbly, black mote.

As he fell, he saw Sir Mantis catch the harpoon, and he knew Jagger would not have time to turn his bike and get him in time, but right at that moment.....THUD! Charlie felt a jolt as his body suddenly changed directions, and went from falling to flying sideways. He soon realized he was in the arms of Professor Hootie.

"We better get to the ship," the professor said, and Charlie nodded in agreement. He could see more Wermuths riding dragons heading toward them.

"Marvin," Jagger spoke into his wristband, "we're going to need you to come pick us up, little buddy. In a hurry!" he emphasized.

They flew toward where they parked the ship. Charlie looked back toward the castle and saw a herd of at least thirty Wermuth driven dragons flying after them. Suddenly, like a thing of beauty, the Lady Alabama appeared above the treetops. It headed right for them and just before reaching the crew members, it spun around with the back end facing them and the hydraulic ramp open. The crew quickly flew into the rear of the ship and the door was immediately closed. The Wermuths on their dragons pulled up short of the impressive craft and stared in amazement. Then, right before their eyes the ship almost vanished as it lifted out of their atmosphere with a blink.

Chapter 13

The Clue from Trikre

(32 hours left)

Back safely on the ship and once again in outer space, the crew caught its breath. Finally Jagger spoke up first and addressed Charlie, "Dude, what were you thinking? You could have gotten us all killed."

"I'm sorry, guys. I know it was stupid, but I just couldn't help myself. I thought about her," Charlie nodded toward Lizzie, still seeming to sleep so peacefully suspended in air, "and I thought 'How long is this charade going to take?', and I just went for it. I just didn't want to waste the time. We don't have it to waste. We don't even know how many more clues there are."

The others seemed to understand, but Dr. Fox spoke up next, "Jagger's right, though, Charlie. You cant go all 'loose cannon' on us. Someone could get hurt, and by my estimation that little stunt of yours did cost us a good hour and a half or so."

Charlie knew she was right, and he felt bad for putting her in danger, for wasting time, for everything. He hung his head, then he heard Jagger say, "Okay, sport, spill the beans. What was that back there? I mean, I've never seen anyone move like that before; fight like that before." He paused. "You some kind of super hero or somethin'?" he joked.

This brought Charlie out of his funk and made him chuckle and grin. He replied, "No, man. Nothing like that."

"So?" Jagger persisted, "What's your story?"

"Okay, so I may have won a couple of martial arts championships."

"Oh yeah," replied Addison, "like high school state championships?"

"Northern Hemisphere." Charlie responded quietly trying not to sound proud.

"Oh snap," exclaimed Jagger which Charlie found ironic coming from a turtle-man, "My man here is like the toughest dude on half the planet. I mean seriously guys, you should have seen the kid in action. He was like 'Wah',"Jagger began a bad impression of Charlie fighting the Wermuths, "and 'Yah' and 'Kerpam'."

"Well," Dr. Fox interrupted, "I did also want to tell you 'Thank you', you know, for saving me back there. That was really brave of you and you almost died because of it."

"And, Professor," said Charlie," I wanted to tell you the same. If you hadn't been there, I don't think I would have made it."

Professor Hootie sat there shaking his head, and he finally spoke, "But what does it all matter. We lost the harpoon, and with it the next clue, and with that, I'm afraid our mission is done," he paused and tried to keep from getting choked up, then finished, "I'm afraid your sister doesn't stand much of a chance. I'm sorry, my boy." He reached out and put his hand on Charlie's knee to console him.

Quickly, Charlie spoke up, "Well I'm not! You don't think I carried that stupid stick around for an hour without reading it do you?"

The Professor and the other crew members became filled with joy. Marvin began patting his chest and producing a bass thumping sound like he was in some night club. "Well, let's hear it, my boy!" exclaimed Professor Hootie.

"It simply said '**Crimson orb omelet feathered friends**'," stated Charlie. "I searched the entire harpoon, and those were the only words on the thing."

"Chuckie-boy, are you sure you're remembering things clearly? I mean you were a bit preoccupied," stated Jagger.

But, Professor Hootie smirked and said to himself, but loud enough for the rest of them to hear him, "Hm, that clever, little Muzz Bug."

"So you understand it?" Charlie asked relieved.

"Well," started the professor, "in the Wermuth language the words are a phrase that mean 'Weapon of great power and honor', fitting to be written on the Legendary Dragon Harpoon of Sir

146

Grottus, but in English, it is the clue we were looking for." He paused and studied the faces which were staring at him in anticipation, then he finished, "Jagger, Marvin, set our course for Aviotto. I'm going home!"

As they flew the eight hour trip to Aviotto, the professor continued to explain that on his planet there were several relics which were adored by his people. One was the Emerald Talon of Caracara, another was the Floating Golden Nest of Lake Condor, and one was the Ruby Egg of Mount Cassowary, the latter of which he felt the clue referred to as a 'crimson orb'. He did state he was a bit confused though, because he knew this relic well and was not aware of any markings on it. The professor told the crew he had grown up in the village at the base of Mount Cassowary, so not only was he going to his home planet, but also his home.

CHAPTER 14

AVIOTTO AND THE RUBY EGG

(24 HOURS LEFT)

As they flew in they could see the mountain which was shaped like the head of a Cassowary bird, complete with a horn-like structure on top. Marvin landed Lady Alabama in a field just outside of a forest of the largest redwood trees Charlie had ever seen. The crew deboarded, and this time, since they knew they were on a friendly planet, Marvin came along. They walked into the forest and Professor Hootie said, "Welcome to Aviotto, and welcome to Owlville."

149

Jagger looked around at the bases of the huge trees, and said, "No offense, Doc, but this place isn't really 'happening'."

"Au contraire," stated Professor Hootie, "I would beg to differ," and with that he motioned toward the treetops. The crew members' eyes went upward and they saw what appeared to be an infrastructure of intricate bridges and houses over fifteen stories up. The bridges were like roadways that linked all the treetops together with multiple huts in each tree at different levels. They could see multicolored Aviottians walking and flying all around. The professor explained that this being Owlville, most all the Aviottians they would encounter would look much like him, only different colors. The crew marveled at the site above them, then finally Addison asked, "So, how do we get up there?"

The professor grinned, then flew about twenty feet up a tree that Charlie noticed was a little bit bigger in diameter than the other trees. Dr. Hootie looked down at the others, and replied with a smirk, "You have to be invited." He then pulled on a branch which bent like a lever and suddenly a door opened at the base of the larger tree. The crew looked up at him with puzzled amazement, and he said, "What? Our flightless friends have to have a way to come visit?" The four crew members stepped inside the tree, Professor Hootie pushed the branch back up, the door closed, and an elevator carried the crew up, up, up, to the village in the treetops.

When the door of the tree reopened, Professor Hootie was standing there waiting on them. They stepped out onto one of the many walkways secured up in the large redwoods.

"Professor," Charlie began, "not to be rude, but... this is really cool and all, and I know you want to show us your home, but the clock is ticking, so why are we here and not on top of Mount Cassowary."

"Good question, my boy, and I promise it's not to walk down memory lane. The reason we are here is that we need the key."

"The key? What key?" Charlie responded.

"About fifty years ago an Aviottian from Crow Island stole the Ruby Egg, but a week later it was retrieved and brought home to its rightful resting place. But, in order to keep this sort of thing from happening again, we Owlvillians, as protectors of the egg, built a gate for the front of the cave in which the egg sits. The mayor of Owlville, keeps the key. So we are going to the mayor's office."

The crew followed the professor across the bridges and passed many huts and owl-like

Aviottians. They could not help but feel out of place, as everyone they passed stopped what they were doing and stared at the foreigners. Then from a hut they had just passed a female Aviottian emerged quickly and exclaimed, "Gordon? Gordon Hootie, is that you?"

Professor Hootie quickly turned around with delight on his face. "Darla," he said before he had completely turned. Jagger and Addison looked at each other and raised their eyebrows at one another, not saying a word, but both saying the same thing with their eyes, "The professor's got a girlfriend." Jagger then looked at Marvin, who put both his hands over his heart and quietly began making a beating heart sound while pumping his hands in and out.

After a long hug and exchanging pleasantries, Darla asked, "So, how long you home for, Gordon? We sure miss you around here. I was hoping we could catch up a bit."

"Oh, Darla," Gordon replied, "I would love nothing more than that, but we are on a mission. A mission that is very time critical, so unfortunately, sweet Darla, I will be leaving again very soon."

Darla's eyes showed she understood this must be a serious situation, but the rest of her body language screamed her disappointment. Then she asked, "Is there anything I can do to help?"

"We are actually on our way to the mayor's office to get the key for the gate to the Ruby Egg. Who *is* the mayor these days?" the professor asked.

Darla's eyes once again said volumes with the concerned look on her face, as she spoke the name, "Theodore Chordata."

"You have to be kidding me. Theo Chordata is the mayor of Owlville?" he stated.

"And I hate to tell you, Gordon," said Darla, "but he doesn't give that key out to just anyone, and when he does he usually goes with them."

"Who's this Theo guy?" asked Jagger.

"Ah, Theodore Chordata was a guy I grew up with. You might say he was somewhat of a bully. This might be hard to believe, but I was a little bit of a nerd when I was in high school. And Theo, loved picking on me, not to mention he had the hots for Darla here. But one day, I decided I'd had enough of the bullying and when Theo got in front of the school to give his speech for the Student Government president, I changed his speech on the teleprompter he was using and his speech made him sound like a fool and the whole school laughed at him. I'd humiliated him."

"Well," Jagger said, "not bad enough to keep him from running for public office, I guess."

"Is this going to be a problem, Professor?" asked Charlie.

"Uh… surely not. I mean, that was thirty-eight years ago," said the professor unconvincingly.

"So, I can help," said Darla. "I'm coming with you to talk to Theo. I mean Mayor Chordata. You really need to call him Mayor Chordata. He really prefers that."

The six of them were now back on their way to see the mayor. They reached a hut after just a few more trees, which had a sign that read "Mayor Theodore E. Chordata". Darla knocked at the door and was answered with a, "You may enter." Darla went in first and the others filed in behind her. A mean looking owl-man with black and red feathers and a bright yellow beak peered up from the desk where he was sitting. Charlie noticed he was sitting in the same nest-chair that Professor Hootie was sitting in the first time he'd met him. To Charlie, this made Theodore Chordata a little less intimidating. The mayor's eyes welcomed Darla quickly, barely looked at Professor Hootie, then fixed on the foreigners with suspicious disdain.

Darla spoke, "Good day to you, Mayor Chordata." His eyes moving back to Darla. "Look who is home and needs your help." Darla motioned to Professor Hootie and the professor moved forward from behind Darla. The mayor studied the owl-man standing in front of him for a few seconds, trying to jar his memory. Then it hit him, and a smirk came over his face.

"Well, well, P.P. Hootie, has returned home," mocked the mayor.

"It's P. Gordon Hootie, and it's good to see you, too, Theo."

"It's Mayor Chodata, and I never said it was good to see you," stated the mayor. "And to what do I owe this visit? The lovely Darla, seems to think you need my help."

Darla spoke up, "They need the key, Theo."

"Mayor," corrected the mayor.

"Mayor," Darla repeated to correct herself.

His face really got suspicious looking now. "The key? Why do you need the key? And, do you really think I'd give it to you? Or, more so, to you and a group of aliens? Yeah, I don't think so."

"Look, Theo," Professor Hootie started and stopped himself, "Mayor Theo. We don't have a lot of time. You see this young man here," the professor grabbed Charlie's arm and pulled him to the front of the group so he could be seen better, and he continued, "... this boy's sister is going to die within 24 hours if we don't save her. Now we have flown across four galaxies and have been to five planets in order to try to save her, and our journey has brought us here and we need to see the Ruby Egg." The professor was on a roll and he continued with confidence, "I know we've had our differences in the past, and I'm sorry if what I did made you feel bad, but that was a long time ago and we are both adults now and we need to act like adults and do the responsible thing here to help save this girl. Besides, this boy," he points again to Charlie, "may seem like just a boy, but he is also a master in the martial arts and very, very driven to save his sister. So, Theo, you can give us the key like the responsible adult you should be at this point in your life, or I'll let my young friend here convince you himself," and the professor almost gasped for air after seemingly saying all that in one breath.

There was a short pause while Mayor Chordata digested all that had just been said, and then he reached into his desk drawer, pulled out a large steel key, and pushed it across his desktop.

"Just wanted to hear you say you were sorry, is all," mumbled Theo, with his head down as to avoid eye contact.

The professor grabbed the key, and said, "Thanks, Mayor Chordata." As they left the office, Darla gave the defeated looking mayor a kiss on the cheek, which seemed to lift his spirits a bit.

As they left out, Charlie asked, "What's the quickest way up the mountain?"

Professor Hootie replied, "We need transport," and he gave Darla a look.

"I'm on it," she said, and she quickly flew up a level and over one tree, and returned with two younger looking male Aviottians who had the exact same blue, purple, and green feather pattern. "This is Burt and Curt," she said, "They are good, strong fliers and they are going to help us with transportation today."

The four non-Aviottians looked a little confused, and the professor said, "Well time's a wasting," and he flew up, grabbed Charlie around the shoulders with his talon-esque feet and lifted him off the elevated boardwalk. Next, Darla did the same with Dr. Fox, and Burt with Jagger, and Curt with Marvin. Before they knew it, they were soaring above the giant redwoods, toward Mount Cassowary.

Once they reached the mountain, they landed on a flat area at what would be the left eye of the bird head shaped mountain. This "eye" was a cave which was blocked off by a large, sturdy steel gate. Charlie thought to himself, "Glad we got the key." Through the thick rungs of the gate, Charlie could see that the entire cave had a red tint, and he spotted the Ruby Egg, about the size of a watermelon with the smaller end pointed up, nestled in a sort of stone goblet,.

Professor Hootie turned to Charlie, holding out the steel key, and said, "Would you like to do the honors?" Charlie, reaching for the key, saw it to be about eight inches long, with a design on the end that looked like owl eyes. He took the key, walked to the lock, and holding the key by the owl eyes, inserted it into the lock. With a turn, the gate opened. The group quickly went to the egg and surrounded it, but no one dared to touch it. Sunlight came through a sky light in the cave and hit directly on the center tip of the egg, which is what caused the red illumination of the space. They examined the egg from every angle they could with it sitting in its stone perch, but they could see no words. They began to examine the goblet it was perched on, but the only words they found there were "The Ruby Egg of Aviotto". They then turned their attention to the walls of the cave, but could find nothing. The eight of them continued to examine the scene, when all of a sudden Curt shouts out, "I found something!" Everyone turned to look in eager anticipation. Curt was back at the gate, and he read what he had found, "It says 'NO TRESPASSING'."

Everyone sighed with disappointment, and Professor Hootie responded, "My dear boy, that sign was put there twenty years ago. We are looking for something that was written about 2,000 years ago."

"There must be something we're missing, Professor," said Dr. Fox frustrated.

"But what?" the professor responded.

Jagger chimed in, "I've got no idea, but I sure could go for one of those omelets about now."

"Hush your mouth," said Darla, put off by the comment. "That's called cannibalism around here."

"Hey, turtles lay eggs, too," retorted Jagger, "but a good omelet... well, that's hard to beat."

"Wait a minute," Charlie interrupted. "Why did you say that? Why did you bring up an omelet?"

"You know," Jagger answered, "The clue. Crimson orb omelet."

"That's right," said Charlie getting excited, "and we all just thought the word 'omelet' was meant to lead us to 'egg', but what if 'orb' is all we needed to get us to 'egg', and 'omelet' is telling us what we should do with it?"

Darla jumped in and said, "But surely you aren't implying that we crack open a two millennia old rel..."

But before she could finish her sentence, they heard a loud "tink" and turned toward the Ruby Egg, where Marvin stood holding the egg still after having just tapped it a bit on the edge of the stone goblet. Nothing happened. Marvin shrugged his shoulders, then raised the egg higher for another go at it, everyone but Charlie yelled, "No!", but it was too late the purple man slammed the side of the Ruby Egg against the stone once more, but this time the "tink" was much louder and... the egg cracked. A crack started right in the center of the egg, but in amazement the group watched as the crack spread over about thirty seconds in a perfect line around the very center of the egg. When the crack ran the full circumference of the egg and reached its starting point, a small puff of steam released from the egg. Charlie raced over to Marvin just as the two sides popped apart, revealing a smaller ruby egg inside. Charlie took from Marvin the large ended side of the egg which contained the new, smaller egg. He set it back in its goblet perch and removed the small egg (which was the size of a normal household egg) from its core. Examining the new egg for words or a clue, he noticed it was scored around its center, duplicating the crack which appeared on the original Ruby Egg. Charlie tried to pull the two pieces apart but they would not separate. He thought about trying to crack this one open as well, but just before he hit it against the stone, he stopped, looked at the egg closely, then gave it a twist. The egg unscrewed into two pieces, and inside he pulled out a small piece of cloth which he read aloud to the group, "**In the center of the City there is a center where there are no worries. Go to the center of that center.** P.S. Please put me back together."

Jagger came over to Charlie and snapped a picture of the piece of cloth then Charlie placed it back inside the small egg and tightened the top down on it. He then placed it back inside the bottom, larger half of the egg which was in its place in the stone goblet. Marvin then walked over and flipped the top, smaller piece of the original Ruby

Egg over and set it on the other piece. Then, again with total amazement, the eight of them watched as a bright, sparkling light, like that of a sparkler held by a child on the 4th of July, retraced the the line of the crack. As the light moved around the egg, the crack line disappeared as if the Ruby Egg was welding itself back together. When the sparkling light reached its origination spot, it fizzled out. All of them walked back to the egg, examined it closely, and could detect no line whatsoever.

"Remarkable," whispered Professor Hootie.

"You can say that again," said Jagger.

The silence of the awe was interrupted as they heard the "Nnt nnt nnt" bass sounds and all looked up at Marvin, who was pretending to be riding a horse, almost like dancing.

"My buddy over there says it's time to go," said Jagger.

And with that the four non-Aviottians were flown straight to their ship by their four feathered friends. Gordon said good-bye to Darla and promised her he would return soon. Marvin and Jagger assumed their driving positions, and the Lady Alabama once again took to the skies.

CHAPTER 15

THE CLUE IN THE RUBY EGG

(16.5 HOURS LEFT)

Once out of Aviotto's atmosphere and into space, Jagger pushed a button on his camera and the image he'd taken of the clue shown all around the ship. Charlie commented first, "He seems to like the word 'center'."

"Ahh, right you are," said Dr. Hootie, "That is because it is an important piece of the clue. A defining piece."

"Ok, so I think I have this one," said Jagger.

"By all means," the professor replied, "let's hear it."

Jagger started, "Ok, so it says 'City', right, and that's like the only word capitalized which I think means that is telling us which planet. But then also there is the repetition of the word 'center' which my main man Chuck just pointed out, and I think that is also telling us which planet, right?" The Professor nodded in approval of his assessment so far, as the others just listened almost seeming more confused. Jagger continued, "So, there is a planet in this system that I'd say I go to more than any other. It's probably one of my most visited planets of all the systems. The entire planet is one big, giant island city with oceans surrounding it. And it is called, get this, Nucleus. Which means, the center of something, whether its a cell or a circle."

"In fact," Professor Hootie interrupted, "the people of Nucleus named it such only about 2500 years ago. Before that it was named Squank, but the people of the planet made a decision to change its name because they said they were the geographical center of Galaxy 9, System 7, which IS accurate, and because they felt they were the financial, technological, and trade center for the entire universe, which actually is not far off, either."

"That's a good call," said Jagger, "Don't think I'd want to tell people I was from a planet called 'Squank'."

"Yeah, like Conchu is so much better," Addison mocked, giving Jagger a grin.

"Hey, I resent that," he responded acting as if his feelings were hurt. "Conchu is a beautiful name for a planet. Conchu," he said and repeated, "Conchu."

"Bless you," Addison joked, as if Jagger was sneezing.

They all chuckled, then Charlie asked, "So, Professor, you think Nucleus is where we need to head?"

"Indeed."

"So what about the rest of the clue? Where on Nucleus do we go? The center of it, I suppose?"

"Indeed," the professor once again responded. "I believe that the second and fourth use of the word 'center' does not mean 'the middle', but more indicates like a shopping center, but in this case not, a shopping center, but instead a park."

"A park?" asked Dr. Fox, like something in her brain just got jarred. "Do you mean Hakuna Matata Park?"

The professor winked at her and said, "It means 'no worries'."

"Aaah, come on guys," Jagger chirped, "y'all are stealing my thunder. I knew that one. Shoot, I visit there almost every time I go to Nucleus. Yep, been there done that."

"So let's go," Charlie urged.

"Chillax, Chuck. Already are. We've been heading that way since we stepped on the ship. I knew I had this one," Jagger said with confidence.

Charlie tried to do just that. He had heard of Nucleus and knew of it being one big city. He knew of the advanced technology that was created and manufactured there. He had heard of kids moving to Nucleus after graduating college to get jobs, but he had not ever really heard about this Hakuna Matata Park.

"Tell me about this park," Charlie said with curiosity.

The Professor started, "Well, the people who live on Nucleus work hard, but they also play hard."

"And by hard," Jagger chimed in, "he means extreme! Hakuna Matata Park IS in the 'center' of the city and it is a skate park two miles in diameter. It's got quarter pipes half pipes, full pipes, loopty loos, fishbowls, pump bumps, rails, spines, launch boxes, angled bowls, hubba ledges, you name it they've got it. All different heights and all different sizes."

"Wow, Dr. Fox, sounds like you ought to move to Nucleus. Bet their emergency rooms stay packed with injuries from this park," stated Charlie wittily.

"Actually, Charlie," Addison replied, "there are no injuries." Charlie looked puzzled.

Jagger jumped back in, "That's right, Chuck. You see this energy technology that is keeping your sister suspended in air? You know, the same technology used for your seats and seat belts? Well that technology was developed on Nucleus a long time ago, and they used it throughout the park, so that anytime someone crashes or falls, a field of energy keeps them from getting injured. Hence the 'no worries' theme of the park. In fact, Lady Alabama here was designed and manufactured on Nucleus," he paused and chuckled to himself, and then said, "Hey Doc, I guess you got to visit home last planet and Lady here gets to come home this go round."

"So we need to go to the center of the park, I guess," said Charlie, "Do you know what is there?"

"I think so. I'm not positive about this, but I think in the very center of the park is the large double-bowl that the locals refer to as the Super Bowl," he paused as he realized the phrase "Super Bowl" meant something else on Earth, but he then continued, "Yeah, I know, right? But it is essentially a large bowl hovering off the ground with another bowl of equal size upside down hovering over the top of it. That's where I think we go."

"Great! How close do you think you can park us?" asked Charlie.

"Oh no. No, no, no. Nucleus has VERY regulated air space. We will be told which of their eight airports to land at and then we'll have options on how we want to make our way into the heart of the city." The flight to Nucleus took the crew about two and a half hours.

Chapter 16

Nucleus, the City Planet

(14 hours left)

As they began their approach to Nucleus, Jagger pushed a button and in a much more professional voice than they had been used to hearing, said, "This is Captain Jagger Jones flying the ship Lady Alabama, number R88T77R. We are requesting to land."

A voice came over the speaker system of the ship and said, "Roger that, Captain Jones. We have confirmation of you visiting with us before, and we are sending you to Airport Northeast."

"Roger that and thank you, sir," replied Jagger. Charlie and Dr. Fox looked at each other and slightly giggled at how formal Jagger was acting. They had never seen this side of him.

"Welcome back to Nucleus," the voice said.

Jagger pushed the button again to cut off the communication between the two. He heard the chuckles behind him and knew what it was about, "Hey, I know how to act when I need to, and I do not want to get on the bad side of   the N.A.S.T.A.S."

"N.A.S.T.A.S.?" questioned Charlie.

"Yeah, the Nucleus Air, Space, and Trade, Association and Security," answered Jagger.

"Thanks, Captain Jones!" Charlie said trying to imitate the voice from the intercom, which got a laugh out of the rest of the crew, including Jagger. Even he thought "Captain Jones" sounded funny when referring to him.

As the Lady Alabama entered Nucleus's atmosphere, the "City" came immediately into view.

Skyscrapers, factories, roads, signs, lights, and colors as far as the eye could see. From the sky, It was an intertwining of concrete, steel, glass, and neon that Charlie had never laid eyes on. Jagger steered the ship toward the Airport Northeast. Nearing the airport, Charlie could barely make out the surrounding ocean a few miles past where they would be landing.

Another voice came over the speaker, "Lady Alabama, you are clear for landing."

"Roger that," Jagger replied and he and Marvin brought the ship straight down onto a landing pad at the Airport Northeast. When they had landed, Jagger pulled his laser gun out of his boot and put it in a compartment near his captain's chair. The crew, minus Marvin, once again exited the ship. Airport security was waiting and escorted them into a room where each crew member was put through a quick full body digital scan, and then they were questioned about their purpose for visiting the planet. Jagger just told security it was a pleasure trip, and that his friends had never been to Hakuna Matata Park and were wanting to visit it. He knew the truth would have been fine, but also knew it would have taken longer to explain as well as trying to respect the privacy of the Muzz Bugs and the anti-venom.

Once they were cleared, Jagger said, "So, how should we travel? Nucleus has a fast monorail system which can get us to the park in 45 minutes or so. Up until about fifteen years ago this is how everyone on Nucleus traveled, but then they developed teleportation. Now there are teleportation stations located throughout the city. So, we can go from here to the heart of the city almost instantaneously."

"Uh," started Charlie, "how do you think we want to travel? Fastest way possible. Teleportation it is."

"Well, actually," said Professor Hootie, "I don't really think you guys will need me so much on this trip, so maybe I'll just stay at the ship."

"Professor," asked Dr. Fox, "are you afraid of teleportation?"

"Call me old fashioned," responded the professor, "but having my molecules broken down in one place and completely reassembled in another is not my idea of fun travel. I think I'll stick to flying, walking, or riding. But don't let me hold you up. I completely understand the time crunch we are in. Jagger knows the 'city' and virtually everyone here speaks English or has a built in auditory translator, so I'll just slow you guys down anyhow."

If not for the issue of time, Charlie thought the professor's statement made a lot of sense and he, too, probably would have chosen the monorail. But, saving Lizzie was the only thing of importance at this point, and all fears were pushed aside. They said bye to the professor and he walked back to the ship to stay with Marvin and Lizzie. The other three walked quickly to the nearest teleportation station. Charlie glanced at his watch which read **13:15:56**.

The airport's teleportation station was essentially a wall with a row of twenty capsules, similar to phone booths, but with no glass. Above ten of the capsules was a sign that said "Coming" and above the other ten, a sign that said "Going". The "Coming" capsules were a neon green color and the "Going" capsules were a neon orange color. They were only big enough for one person to get in at a time. There was a line of different beings at each of the "Going" capsules about seven people deep, but the lines moved pretty quickly. The three of them got in different lines across from each other.

"I think it'll be pretty self explanatory as to what to do once you get inside," stated Jagger who was in a line between Charlie and Addison. Both of their heads quickly turned toward him and all three took another step forward.

"Wait a minute," said Addison, "you've never done this before?"

"Nah, I've always opted for the monorail. You heard the doc, it's a little freaky. Besides, the city is kinda pretty to ride through." All three got just a little more nervous each time they saw the light glowing from the cracks of the orange capsules and then with each move forward. But, each time they saw someone exit the green capsules they were slightly comforted, and finally they all entered the capsules at the same time.

When Charlie closed the capsule door behind him, a holographic face of a lady appeared and said, "Hello, where would you like to go today?"

Charlie quickly replied, "Hakuna Matata Park."

He then braced for teleportation, but instead the voice came back on and said, "We have four stations at Hakuna Matata Park. Which one would you like to travel to Station North, South, East, or West?"

Charlie panicked, they hadn't discussed which station, but he felt pressured. He didn't know if the others were gone yet or not. He didn't know if he could cancel or not. This was all new to him, so he just said the first thing that popped into his mind, "North."

The voice came on one more time and said, "Thank you. Have a nice trlp."

The capsule was filled with a bright light, and then the light dimmed. Charlie heard another voice, a man's voice this time, say, "Welcome to North Hakuna Matata Park. Please exit the teleportation capsule immediately."

Charlie did just that. He could hardly believe he'd gone anywhere, but when he stepped out, he saw a sign that read "Hakuna Matata Park: Don't Worry, Be Reckless", and he glanced back over his shoulder to see a neon green capsule. He quickly looked around and there he saw Addison. She smiled at him and he ran to her and hugged her.

"North." she said smiling, "Glad somebody thinks like I do." They decided to wait for five minutes, to see if Jagger would show up after having gone to one of the other stations. They realized they had no phones or radios with them to try to reach him. Jagger had his wristband, which kept them in touch with the ship, but they really hadn't planned on getting separated from him.

After the five minutes, Charlie said, "Well, we are all going to the same place, so let's just get to the Super Bowl as fast as we can."

As they turned to start to jog through the park, Charlie saw beings from a multitude of different planets riding "thruster-boards" all over the place. They were doing some of the coolest tricks on some of the steepest ramps he'd ever laid eyes on, and none of them were even wearing helmets, but none were getting hurt, even though plenty were falling. The park's tracks, ramps, jumps, bowls, rails, etc... were all made of different neon colors; pinks, oranges, yellows, blues, greens, purples, and reds everywhere.

"Thruster-boards?" Charlie questioned. "He never said anything about thruster-boards."

Thruster-boards were like snow boards with built in thrusters that the driver controlled with a small remote they held in their hand. "I've only heard myths of their existence, but the technology ban on Earth has never allowed them." He pointed to a stand where it appeared the boards were being rented out. "We have to get one," he said, "It'll be quicker."

Dr. Fox rolled her eyes at him and said sarcastically, "Right. It'll be quicker," thinking this kid just wants to have a little fun. But she agreed and they went to the stand.

The clerk working at the thruster-board stand was a short, plump male creature with blue scales, one eye, and a miniature elephant trunk. He seemed uninterested in the two humans walking toward him.

Charlie spoke first, "Two thruster-boards, please."

"That'll be twenty makas," he said as if he was being bothered by the request. He then reached into a bucket sitting on the counter and dropped something into his mouth, underneath his truck, that looked like some sort of meat ball.

"We only have dollars," stated Addison.

"Oh, must be from Galaxy 5. I can convert, no problem. He touched one of his three fat fingers to a computer screen and then said, "Okay, that'll be one thousand seven hundred dollars." Addison emptied her pockets but only found two five hundred dollar bills. Charlie had nothing. He had not planned to spend any money when he left the house to go bike riding with his sister about fifty-eight hours ago.

"We only have a thousand," said Addison.

"Then I guess you'll just get one board," said the blue salesman as he popped another meat ball into his mouth.

"That won't do," said Charlie to Dr. Fox. "We need two boards, we have a mile to go to get to the..."

Just then Charlie was interrupted by a wheezing sound. He and Addison looked back at the salesman who appeared to be choking on one of the meat balls he was eating.

"We have to help him," Dr. Fox said, "I have to get to him." The window of the stand was not big enough for either of them to fit through. They quickly ran around the small building and found a door on the back side, but it was locked.

"Back up," Charlie ordered Dr. Fox. He then did a spinning side kick and almost completely unhinged the door. They both ran inside the thruster-board stand and by the time they got to him, the scaly blue being was unconscious on the floor lying face up.

"Quick," Addison began, "help me get him rolled over."

"Shouldn't we try to get the food out," asked Charlie while doing what he was asked.

"It's too late for that," said Dr. Fox. "I need to create an airway below the obstruction now."

"Then why are we rolling him over," questioned Charlie again.

"He is a Kelf, most likely originally from the planet, Frenkle, in Galaxy 8, System 4. They have a hard flat bone that is impenetrable from the front, but their trachea runs more toward their backs anyway," by this point they had the Kelf rolled onto his stomach and Addison was looking around for something she could use to puncture through the Kelf's back and into his trachea. After seeing nothing of use on the counters around her, she remember the clicking ink pen that she had clipped to the inside of her shirt. She took it out, unscrewed it from the middle, and removed the spring, the clicker, and the writing apparatus from the pen leaving it hollow. She then screwed the two pieces back together and quickly thrust the pen into the Kelf's back with a hard downward blow. The pen penetrated the trachea. Dr. Fox his back, and immediately air was able to get to the Kelf's lungs, and he awakened with a gasp. They sat the Kelf up, and seeing a red "Emergency" icon on the salesman's computer screen, Charlie pushed it.

"I'm sorry about this, sir," said Charlie being careful of his words, "but we really are in a bit of a hurry, and help is on the way. Do you think that..."

The Kelf interrupted him with a weak out of breath voice, "Go. You take two boards. Any two you like. No charge. I thank you."

Charlie looked at Dr. Fox to see if it was alright, and she nodded, knowing her patient was going to be okay. They grabbed two thruster-boards with remote controls and headed out.

Once back in the park they dropped their boards and jumped on. Charlie felt guilty about the excitement he was feeling with Lizzie just lying in the ship, not knowing what the future held for her, and knowing how much she'd like to be riding a thruster-board alongside of him. But nonetheless, he was excited and he took off, pushing the thrust button on his remote at all times in order to keep top speed. It didn't take him long to get the hang of it. Charlie was a great athlete and very coordinated, plus he'd skate boarded and snow boarded his entire life. Addison, on the other hand, took a little more time to get the hang of it, but she kept up with Charlie the best she could, trying not to slow him down.

There was no flat, straight path through the park to the Super Bowl, so the two of them were trying to stay in as straight of a path as possible, but were going over ramps, through tunnels, down rails (well, Addison skipped the rails), and in and out of long winding swimming pool like bowls, but always toward the heart of the park. Before long, Charlie could see it. It stood apart from everything in the park not only in its physical uniqueness, but also in that every other element in the park was painted a bright neon color, and the Super Bowl was white and white only. A sleek white, much like Lady Alabama. It was placed exactly one mile into the park, and when it came into Charlie's view it got his adrenaline really pumping and he began to leave Dr. Fox behind a bit. He had built up so much speed as he approached it that he came off a ramp, and was about to slam into the Super Bowl itself when he quickly leaped from his board to the side, and prepared his body for a hard impact with the ground, but there was not one. Charlie rolled, but it was like he'd hit a lightweight air mattress that gave with his body and kept him from hitting the ground.

He stood up and to himself whispered, "No worries." He then looked at the object if front of him in awe. It was two bowls which, kind of came together to make a ball. A ball that was forty feet in diameter, with a crease in the middle about a yard tall where the two pieces didn't touch, in which you could catch a glimpse of a thruster-board whiz by every few seconds. The bottom half, or lower bowl, seemed to be floating about six feet off the ground, and the top half, or upper/upside down bowl, seemed to hover over top of it about three feet. As Charlie, finished marveling at the object, he then began trying to figure out how to get into it. Addison, finally arrived as well, and she, too marveled. Then she asked, "So how do we get in? Or do we?"

About that time, a door in the direct bottom of the lower bowl opened, creating a ramp with which you could ride your boards up. All of a sudden a head popped out of the opening upside down. It was a turtle head. It was Jagger.

"What took you guys so long?" he said with a grin.

Charlie and Addison both smiled and were relieved to be reunited.

"Which..." Addison began, but was quickly interrupted by Jagger.

"West," he said proudly. "C'mon, you should have known... the wild, wild, west." Addison just rolled her eyes.

Then Jagger said, "I searched out there pretty well before coming inside, but I think what we're looking for is in here," and he motioned for them to come in. Charlie and Dr. Fox hopped back on their boards and up the ramp into the sleek white structure. Once inside, the door closed and seemed to disappear into the rest of the bowl, but the thing that caught Charlie's attention was the floating silver, mirrored ball in the very center of the sphere created by the two bowls. He repeated the clue in his head, "In the center of the City there is a center where there are no worries. Go to the center of that center." This silver, hovering, bowling ball looking sphere was the total center… the absolute heart of the city; the nucleus of Nucleus.

"Yep," Jagger said as he watched Charlie staring at the orb and knowing what he was thinking. "So I made a couple of revolutions around this place, trying to get a look at that thing from all angles, before I saw you two from the window," he pointed to the three foot division between the two bowls, "and there is something etched on the very top of it, I just haven't been able to read it fully yet."

"That has to be the clue. Well let's get to it!" exclaimed Charlie and he began to get his thruster-board revved up in order to circumvent the sphere. As he got to where he was almost completely upside down, he turned his eyes toward the silver ball and he saw the etched words, but couldn't make them out, and like that, he was passed. "Dang it, this is going to be harder than I thought. C'mon guys give me some help here."

Addison and Jagger both started "skating" around the inside of the sphere. The three of them looked like some kind of circus act whizzing around one another, one upside down, one right side up, while the other was almost horizontal, narrowly missing colliding with each other, and each with the same goal of trying to get a glimpse of the words etched on top of the hovering silver ball.

"Check," shouted Addison, as she was the first to read the first word.

Charlie looped back around and shouted out as he read, "the collar. Check the collar."

Jagger passed over the orb and said, "Nothing. I got nothing."

Addison again looped upside down, and was able to catch the next three words, "of the ancient," she said, "Check the collar of the ancient." And they all repeated.

Charlie was flipped upside down and was able to make out the next word, "Giant! Check the collar of the ancient giant!" And the others repeated the phrase.

Jagger flipped and read, "giant, who. Check the collar of the ancient giant, who."

"Slithers deep," read Dr. Fox, obviously the fastest reader of the group. "Check the collar of the ancient giant, who slithers deep."

"In the," Charlie said, "Check the collar of the ancient giant, who slithers deep in the." It was repeated.

Jagger made another go, "Water car, maybe? Not sure on that one," he said.

Addison, who'd seemed to perfect her technique made another run, "Water *cut*," she corrected Jagger, "Check the collar of the ancient giant, who slithers deep in the water cut something," she said. "I think there was just one more word."

Charlie, looking to finish off this clue, made what he hoped was his final revolution around the sphere, and once directly upside down he read and shouted, "CAVES! **Check the collar of the ancient giant, who slithers deep in the water cut caves.**"

They all repeated in unison, "Check the collar of the ancient giant, who slithers deep in the water cut caves." Jagger spoke into his wristband as to record the clue, just in case.

"I've got no clue what that means," said Charlie. "I mean I guess its some big, old, snake wearing jewelry in some caves, but I have no clue where to find that."

"Well," started Dr. Fox, "I have an idea, but I'm pretty sure Professor Hootie will have some answers. Come on, let's go."

"Open," Jagger said and once again the door in the bottom of the Super Bowl opened, and they rode their thruster-boards out. "Which way," asked Jagger.

Charlie answered, "I'd like to go back the way *we*," he pointed to Addison and himself, "came in. Think I'd feel more comfortable retracing my path."

"Due north it is," stated Addison the the three of them took off back through the park.

As they came to the edge of the park and neared the teleportation station, Jagger glanced over at the thruster-board rental stand where there was a medical vehicle hovering with lights flashing on top of it. "Whoa," he said, "looks like somebody had some worries in the no worry zone. Wonder what happened over there?"

Addison cut her eyes at Charlie, and he at hers, both grinned a bit, and Charlie replied, "Don't 'worry' about it."

Jagger saw the funny look the two gave each other and knew they knew more than they were saying. He then glanced back over and saw two men in medical uniforms helping a blue man with a trunk for a nose and something he couldn't quite make out sticking out of the man's upper back. The two men helped the blue man, who was walking on his own, onto the medical vehicle.

Jagger turned to ask Charlie and Addison another question, but then just decided to let it go.

When they got to the line at the teleportation station they conferred this time. "Okay," Jagger said, "We'll be going to 'C station of Airport Northeast'. That's the one we used before and that's the closest to Lady Alabama.

When it was their turn, they each stepped into the orange capsules and five seconds later stepped out of green capsules. They quickly made their way back to the ship, and found Marvin outside with the ramp open, cleaning Lady with a cloth, all while making his beat sounds and dancing.

CHAPTER 17

THE CLUE FROM NUCLEUS

(8 HOURS LEFT)

Back on the ship, Charlie first kissed Lizzie's forehead, and then immediately went to Professor Hootie to share the clue.

"The clue read '**Check the collar of the ancient giant, who slithers deep in the water cut caves',**" announced Charlie.

"We're going to Nangu`n, aren't we?" asked Addison.

"It sure sounds that way," replied Professor Hootie.

"Well alright," said Charlie. "Let's get this baby back up in the air!"

Jagger saluted him and said, "Aye aye, cap'n." And he and Marvin assumed their normal flying positions. Jagger pushed a button and said, "Airport Northeast, this is Captain Jagger Jones with the Lady Alabama, requesting clearance for take off."

A voice resounded back, "Roger that, Captain Jones. Hope you and your crew had a pleasant visit to Nucleus, and you are clear for take off."

"Ten Four on all accounts," replied Jagger and with that they shot up through the atmosphere and were quickly back in space.

"How long until we get to this Nangu`n place?" asked Charlie.

"I'd say about four hours," Jagger answered. "How bout you Marv?" Marvin raised a thumb in the air as to agree with Jagger's estimation.

Charlie turned to Addison, "So how do you know about this Nangu'n planet?"

"A class I took," replied Dr. Fox, "a class that Professor Hootie taught me."

"Ahh," started the professor, swelling with pride, "like I said, you were one of my best students."

"What was the class?" asked Charlie.

Addison thought about it for a second and then answered, "Legends, I think. Was it the Legends course, Professor?"

"Indeed," answered the professor. "Legends of Galaxies 6-10. I haven't taught that course in years," the professors tone changed to a bitter one, "The university said we should stick to more 'factual' courses, so it's mostly Relics, Languages, and Geography these days."

"In fact," Addison said like a light bulb had just gone off in her head, "that's the same course I learned about the Muzz Bugs."

"Indeed," the professor said again.

"So what's the legend with this Nangu`n?" asked Charlie curiously.

"Addison," spoke the professor, "Let's see what you remember?"

"Well, if I recall, Nangu`n is a planet that is essentially a big ball of dirt, with underground rivers that have carved out caves and caverns throughout the planet."

" 'Water cut caves'," whispered Charlie to himself and the professor nodded.

Addison continued, "Legend has it that there is a waterfall at the core of the planet which is where all the rivers branch from, and that there is a sort of 'Guardian of the Waterfall' who is thought to be over four thousand years old."

"And that's the giant snake?" asked Charlie.

"Not a snake," Dr. Hootie jumped in, "Nangu`n is a planet of large earthworms. Very large earthworms. Very large *intelligent* earthworms. But the largest, wisest of all is, Succiah."

"Succiah?" said Charlie confused.

"It means 'father worm'. He is the worm from which all the others originated. The legend says in the planet's origination, it was just a big solid ball of dirt with a small empty space about a foot in diameter as its core. No water and no life. Then one day, about four thousand years ago, in the core of the planet a small waterfall and a small worm appeared. The two began to grow in a kind of symbiosis. As the waterfall got bigger, so did the worm, until one day the water from the waterfall couldn't be contained and it started flowing away creating rivers. At this same point, the now large worm began shedding smaller worms from his body. The new rivers and the new worms both dug into the dirt from the core and began moving toward the surface of the planet. Today, there are holes all over the surface of the planet. These holes are the caves created by the rivers and worms."

"With so many holes, how will we know which one to go in to find this 'ancient giant'?" asked Charlie.

"It is thought," continued the professor, "that each and every hole, though through a labyrinth of caves, would eventually lead you to the core of the planet where the waterfall and Succiah, the 'father worm' or 'ancient giant', reside, since each originated from the two."

"And the collar?" Charlie asked.

"That's a new one for me," admitted the professor, "I wasn't aware Succiah wore a collar, and I'm honestly not sure how he'd even get one, with no arms and and no materials other than water and dirt, but I guess we'll find out. You know, it's all considered 'legend' because there is no record of anyone having gone to Nangu`n in over a thousand years. There's just not much interest for the rest of the world in going to a planet full of worms and holes I guess."

Charlie sighed, he had thought the legend was really pretty cool, but he also thought it sounded like it was going to take a long time, and they were running out of time. "Landing on the planet," he began to express his concern to the others, "walking through no telling how many miles of caves, possibly having to swim across rivers. That will likely take hours, if not days. And what for, just to find another clue, and then have to turn around and find our way back out to find another clue. And how many more clues are there going to be?" his voice grew in frustration and looked down at his watch which read **07:43:15**, and continued quieter, "I don't think we have enough time. I don't think SHE has enough time," and he got up and walked over to Lizzie again. He stood over her, grabbed her hand, and he began to cry. "I'm sorry, sis. I was supposed to look after you. I was suppose to protect you. I let you down."

Addison walked over to him and put her arms around him. She kissed his cheek and said, "C'mon now. We can't give up. YOU can't give up. You can't give up on HER. You've done everything you possibly can to save her, and you know it. There is still hope. Maybe this is the last clue. Maybe the anti-venom is inside Succiah's collar. You don't know, but you can't give up."

"I know," Charlie said wiping away some of his tears, "but even if that's the case, by the time we get to Nangu`n we'll have less than four hours to get to the core of the planet and then get back to the surface with the anti-venom."

Addison tried not to look discouraged, but she also knew he was right. She took her seat again, and Charlie stayed with Lizzie. The rest of the flight to Nangu`n was pretty silent, with each crew member left to their own thoughts.

CHAPTER 18

NANGU`N AND SUCCIAH'S COLLAR

(3:58:24 LEFT)

Nangu`n came into view through the windshield of Lady Alabama, and as described, it looked like a huge ball of swiss cheese mud. This planet didn't have an atmosphere, it just went from space to dirt. They had to slow down as they approached to make sure they didn't crash into it. As they moved closer to the planet, they all gazed at it through the front of the ship. Jagger, checking his coordinates, was hit with a realization, "Game changer!" he shouted.

Charlie didn't understand, but Jagger was revving the ship back up and they started to pick up speed once more. Charlie then realized they were not as close to the planet as he had thought, something Jagger had realized from his coordinates. The ship picked up even more speed as they got even closer to the planet.

"Night goggles!" Jagger shouted and a robot arm placed a set of goggles onto Jagger and Marvin's faces. Then he said, "Oh... Charlie-boy, there will be no walking through miles of caves today, and no swimming across any rivers. We'll be flying this ship all the way to the core!"

And Charlie saw it... the "holes"... they were huge. They were more than big enough for the Lady Alabama to fly into. In this moment, he also regained hope because he realized if what Addison said were true and this was the last clue, and Succiah's collar did contain the anti-venom, then Lizzie would now be with them and they would not have to spend more time trying to reach the surface getting the anti-venom back to her.

The ship reached the planet and whizzed right by the surface into the closest hole there was. "It's not supposed to matter which one, right, doc?" Jagger stated.

"That's what the legend says," retorted Professor Hootie,

Very quickly they were deep into the caves, and complete darkness fell upon them. Jagger steering the ship this way and that, not slowing down a bit. Marvin had started doing his bass sounds from the back of them.

"Got any more of those goggles," asked Dr. Fox. "I feel like I'm getting a little sick not seeing where we are going."

"Oh, right. Sorry about that,"Jagger replied, then shouted, "Passenger night goggles." And all three of the other crew members were distributed goggles.

Still not much could be seen. Mostly what showed up in the goggles were the whitecaps on the raging rivers and every now and then the outline of a large worm on the wall of a cave which all showed up as a tint of green.

"I figure stay just above the water and that should eventually get us there," stated Jagger. It sounded like as good of a plan as any to Charlie, although he might have thrown in the words "and don't crash."

The turns and steep drops as they maneuvered through the caves, felt like they were on a roller coaster, but a roller coaster with no rails. They travelled for miles and miles, up and down, turning left, turning right, staying just above the water always. Charlie pushed the light button on his watch which now read **01:11:45.** This was definitely the longest roller coaster ride he'd ever been on, but finally they saw it. Through their goggles it appeared as a huge wall of green tinted raging water. It was the water fall. Jagger slowed the ship to almost an idle and found some solid ground near the waterfall to land on. Marvin opened the ramp and cut on the exterior lights of the ship which dimly lit the cave they were in. The crew exited the ship holding flashlights to help them see where they were going. Once in the cave they looked around but did not quickly see this worm that was supposed to be so big. Charlie yelled so as to be heard over the crashing waters of the falls, "Hello? Hello, Succiah? We need your help!" he yelled and continued, "My sister, she needs your help. She was stung by a Muzz Bug..."

Before he could say anymore, they heard a rustling and the wall that their flashights shone on began to move. They then heard a strong but calming voice above them say, "How long ago?" All of their flashlights turned quickly upward, and revealed a worm twenty feet in diameter, with one eye in it's center. They were startled, and the worm looking down on them asked again, "Your sister, how long ago was she transfused by the Muzz Bug?"

Charlie stuttered a little, but answered, "It's been about **71 hours**," Charlie said glancing at his watch which now read **00:51:31.**

"Well," said the voice, "I should guess you are going to want to take a look at my collar pretty quickly then."

"Yes sir," Charlie replied. "If it's okay with you?"

Succiah chuckled and slid down further, putting his head closer to theirs, but more importantly putting his collar to a level they could read it. Succiah's collar was black but when their lights shined upon it they saw a gold medallion hanging from it. Charlie was trying to see if there was anyway the medallion could open and contain the anti-venom, but to his disappointment as the medallion came more into focus he could see words written on it — another clue. Charlie's heart dropped. He knew they did not have time to make it to another planet. Charlie dropped his head and put his hands on his knees. He could not even look at the words, because to him, those words represented his defeat and ultimately his sister's death.

Jagger began to read, "**In order for you to cure the lame, they must drink from Mr. Roy Biv's middle name.**" He paused, then said, "That doesn't even make a bit of sense. How in the world are you supposed to drink from a man's middle name."

Professor Hootie chimed in, "This one is challenging. It doesn't seem to point to any planet in particular that I can tell."

"And besides," Jagger started in again with frustration in his voice, "who is this Mr. Roy Biv anyway? And how are we supposed to know some random dude's middle name?"

Charlie was still leaned over with his hands on his knees and his head down. He really hadn't put much thought into the clue, he'd barely even heard it, but the last thing Jagger said registered something in his mind. He spoke lightly, "It's Green."

The others turned toward him. "Do what?" asked Jagger.

"Green," said Charlie a little louder, but still defeated.

"I think you were looking through those goggles too long, Chuck," said Jagger.

Addison walked to him, put her hands on his back, and asked, "What do you mean Charlie? What's green?"

"Mr. Roy Biv's middle name," he answered, "It's Green."

"Wait a minute, kid, are you telling me you know this Roy Biv guy?" said Jagger in disbelief.

"Charlie, my boy," the professor enquired, "how did you come to that conclusion?"

"It's a rainbow. The colors in the rainbow. You know...Roy G. Biv. Red, orange, yellow, green, blue, indigo, and violet. ROY G. BIV."

"Indeed. Indeed!" said the professor realizing he was right.

"But it doesn't matter," shouted Charlie almost coming to tears again, "So we are supposed to get Lizzie to drink something green... but what is it.... and WHERE is it? We don't know where to go and even if we did, we wouldn't have time to get there. We are stuck down here in this cave, and it took us almost three hours to get from the surface here, and now we have to go back to the surface, and..."

And just then an amazing thing happened, Charlie was interrupted, not by sound, but by light. Succiah's body began to glow. It started fairly dim, but continued to get brighter and as it did, more worms stuck to the walls, ceiling, and floor of the cavern began to glow. The crew hadn't even known these other worms were there until now.

"Glowworms," Addison said lightly, as she along with the rest of the crew dropped their jaws open in amazement at the beauty of this event.

"I did not know about that," stated the professor to his pupil.

As the cavern filled with light, they turned their flashlights off, because they were no longer needed, and they began to look around the massive cave. Quickly each of their eyes became fixed on one thing and one thing only; the waterfall. The waterfall they had seen in the dark, the waterfall they'd been hearing crashing down, the waterfall that had produced the rivers of this planet, was not like any other waterfall they'd ever seen. This was a multi-colored waterfall with seven distinct colors flowing through it, spawning seven different colored rivers which ran out of this cavern and through the rest of Nangu`n. The colors from left to right were red, orange, yellow, green, blue, indigo, and violet.

"Nor did I know about that," said the professor in awe.

For Charlie Paige, gazing upon this massive rainbow waterfall in all it's glorious colors, meant hope, and that hope rushed back into his once hopeless body. He looked at his watch, **00:15:11,** and he began to bark orders, "Marvin, I need a bucket or cup or something! Jagger, get out one of the bikes. Dr. Fox, get Lizzie ready, I'm bringing back some anti-venom."

"No need for the bike," Professor Hootie said, "I've got you, son," and he flew up and grabbed Charlie just as he did back on Aviotto. As he raised him off the ground, Marvin emerged from the ship with the first thing he could find that could catch and hold some water, and he threw it up to Charlie. Charlie, a bit surprised at catching a pair of night goggles, realized they would actually work very nicely, and he gave Marvin a thumbs up, and Marvin gave him a thumbs up in return.

The professor flew Charlie toward the center, green portion of the waterfall, but as they got close, water was crashing all around and spraying them. It was hitting their eyes making it difficult to see. The professor's wings were getting wet and heavy, and Charlie's clothes were getting soaked which was making him heavy as well.

"Charlie," yelled the professor over the crashing of the falls, "I don't know if I can hold you much longer," and with that the professor lost his grip on the seventeen year old, and dropped him into the center of the waterfall. Charlie fell about 50 feet, but immediately straightened his body so he'd hit the water toes first. Upon impact, his body was pushed under the water at least 15 feet by the force of the falling water, and the goggles were ripped from his hands and began to sink further. Charlie quickly swam down a few more feet, then away from the falls, but he could not retrieve the goggles. He swam with the green water, and it's current pulled him along.

Jagger, seeing what had happened from the bank, got his flying bike from the ship and sped away to try to catch Charlie before the strong current took him too far. The waters branched into seven rivers very close to the base of the waterfall, and Jagger had not seen which river Charlie had gone down, but he had a pretty good hunch he was in the middle one, the green one.

Jagger reached the green river and saw Charlie's head pop out of the water. Charlie also saw Jagger and he raised one hand to signal him. Jagger flew the bike low to the water and leaned over with one hand reached down and the other steering the bike. Jagger's hand clutched onto Charlie's forearm and Charlie's to his. Jagger steered the bike up and pulled Charlie's body out of the water. With his other hand, Charlie grabbed onto the frame of the bike and pulled himself onto the back of the speedster. Once securely on he checked his watch, **00:02:44.** Jagger saw it, too. He knew there wasn't time for another run, but he knew they'd try. "You okay, buddy," he asked Charlie, and Charlie nodded yes.

They sped back to the bank and the ship. Jagger said, "Get another pair of goggles and we'll go right back out. I'm not sure why you guys went toward the falls in the first place, when you could have just gone to the green river." Charlie knew he was right, but had been in such a hurry he hadn't really thought it through. They landed at the ship and Jagger continued, "Well hurry, and I'll take you back out," but Charlie jumped off the bike and shook his head. Just then, Charlie's alarm on his watch started beeping. He looked down to read **00:00:00** blinking at him. He quickly pushed past Marvin, and saw the professor sitting, trying to catch his breath on the bank. He hurried up the ramp and into the Lady Alabama where he saw Dr. Fox standing with Lizzie. She saw him, and got excited, but then noticed he wasn't carrying any green water, and she asked, "Where's the...?", but before she could finish, Charlie pushed her aside and looked at his sister once more lying there peacefully. Then with his left hand he pinched in on both her cheeks, which caused her mouth to slightly open, he leaned down putting his mouth to hers, and expelled all the green water he could hold in his mouth, into hers. He then closed her mouth, so as to not let any of the water get away, and so it would only have one place to go... into his sister. And he waited.

The other crew members had made their way into the ship, and surrounded Lizzie. They too, waited. Having heard the beeping of his watch alarm, their faces were long and lacking hope. But not Charlie... Charlie's face still had hope.

You see, Charlie knew something the other crew members did not. What he knew was that back at the hospital on Earth, when Dr. Fox had told him about the 72 hour time frame Lizzie had and he set his timer, it had only been an estimate. He remembered he had given around a fifteen minute cushion to his countdown. Close to a minute passed by, the longest sixty seconds of Charlie's life, and then he heard a gurgle. It was the most wonderful sound he'd ever heard. Then another gurgle, which was followed by a gulp, and then a cough. With the second cough, Lizzie's hand actually came up to cover her mouth. Charlie grabbed and clutched her other hand, raised it up and kissed it. Lizzie's eyes blinked, and her head turned toward Charlie and she said weakly, "Oo, gross, you lame-oh."

Charlie smiled, laughed, and cried all at the same time. The rest of the crew did the same.

CHAPTER 19

THE LEGEND, PART 2

Charlie found it quite refreshing NOT to be in a hurry, so after Lizzie awoke, the crew decided to just hang out for a little while on Nangu`n. Charlie filled in the confused Lizzie with the basics of what had happened over the last few days with just the two of them on the ship. Then they walked down the ramp of the Lady Alabama where Charlie introduced his new friends to Lizzie and told her all the ways that they had helped to save her life. They all gathered and sat on crates from the ship on the bank of the rivers in the cavern, which was still illuminated by the numerous large glow worms lining the walls and ceiling. Charlie began by telling

Lizzie the Legend of the Muzz Bug, and he did it almost word for word how he'd heard it from Professor Hootie.

The professor said, "I'm impressed, Charlie, my boy. You may be giving Addison here a run for my top student."

The crew reminisced about the journey and now were able to laugh at some of the things that had occurred. Jagger passed around a big bag of Cheetos as they talked. Lizzie and Succiah listened to the adventures and laughed with the crew. Jagger told about watching Charlie "go ninja" on the Wermuths, Charlie told Lizzie about the funny language of the Semtarians, Professor Hootie told how he had to dodge the Wermuth's spears inside the castle until he could get outside and hide, Charlie talked about seeing Jagger for the first time at the arcade and how "disappointed" he was, and

Jagger finally heard the story about the choking Kelf at the thruster-board stand.

At a point in the conversation, Professor Hootie turned to Succiah and said, "So, Succiah, I have to ask, where did you get that collar? I mean with no arms, and no gold on this planet, am I to assume the 'clue creator' Muzz Bug made it for you?"

"That would be a wise assumption," replied Succiah.

The professor, along with the rest of them, were now very curious, "So you knew him? You knew the Muzz Bug from the legend?" asked the professor.

"You mean Calvin? Well of course I knew him," said Succiah. "You know that part in 'the legend' where it says he stung a 'being from another species'? Well that would be me. That's right, it's been around 2,000 years ago, but I remember it like it was yesterday. I was only a couple of thousand years old at that point and these two Muzz Bugs come flying down in here all recklessly. I was actually hanging out on the ceiling that day when Calvin came flying in. He and his dad were playing some game like tag I think, and it was dark and I blended into the ceiling pretty well, I guess. Anyway, it was a complete accident, but his nose stuck right in my backside. His dad actually caught him, falling toward the waters, and brought him here to the bank. Calvin said his dad never hesitated, but transfused him immediately. As for me, I dropped like a broken stalactite from the ceiling, and landed right in the mouth of the waterfall. I'm guessing there was a splash like you've never seen before, but I wasn't awake for it. So I hit the water and got me a big ol' gulp of 'the green', and within a couple minutes, I was back up and at 'em. Calvin couldn't believe it. He'd never seen a creature survive a muzz infusion except for a dying Muzz Bug. He said he wanted to create this scavenger hunt type thing to honor his dad and maybe save a life at some point. I agreed to it. He told me all the places he was leaving clues, and actually conferred with me on some. The Dragon Harpoon one was my idea. We got to be pretty good friends really. I figured someday someone would show up, and well, I guess today was that day. Calvin would be happy that his dad's life was honored by Miss Lizzie here having new life."

All those present, listened in awe of the story, and Professor Hootie was absolutely giddy to be a student, not a teacher, for a change. The group stayed and chatted with the wise, ancient, giant, glowworm for several more hours, then they re-boarded the ship for the voyage home.

Chapter 20

The Voyage Home

They weaved back through the caves of Nangu`n, but this time at a much slower pace. It took them about six hours but they finally reached the edge of the planet and were once again in space.

Professor Hootie walked up behind Jagger in his normal seat, put his hand on his shoulder and said very seriously, "Captain Jones, would you mind taking me home."

Jagger said, "Sure, doc, I'm taking everyone home."

But Professor Hootie shook his head and said, "No, my real home." Jagger, Addison, and

Charlie realized at this point he meant to Aviotto. "It's where I belong now," continued the professor, and Jagger just nodded and said nothing.

So they flew back to Aviotto. They got out and walked with the professor back to the "elevator tree" in the forest. Charlie pointed to the village up in the huge trees, and was overjoyed that Lizzie was getting to see this. As beautiful as it was the first time, though, Charlie noticed things this trip he hadn't even seen last time. The planet was so much prettier than he'd remembered without the anxiety of Lizzie's possible death looming over him.

They all hugged Professor Hootie and told him good-bye. Charlie gave him an extra long hug and said, "Professor, I can't thank you enough… for everything. We absolutely could not have done this without you. You saved my life on Trikre, but more importantly, you saved my sister. Thank you, sir."

The professor replied, "Oh, Charlie, my boy, I knew as soon as I started talking to you in my office that this was something I was supposed to do. I believe, it was something I was born to do. There has been a reason I stayed on Earth as long as I did, and I believe helping you save your sister was that reason. That's why I now feel at complete peace about coming back home here to Owlville to stay. So, thank you, son. Thank you."

As they turned to head back to the ship, Addison turned back and shouted, "Tell Darla we said 'Hello'."

The professor grinned and said, "Will do," and with that he took off soaring up into the treetops.

Back on the ship, Charlie told Jagger, "There is one more stop I'd really like to make, one more place I'd really like Lizzie to see before we go home." Without even hearing it, Jagger flew them there.

Vroom! Vroom! The bikes revved, as the two teenagers glanced at each other both clutching their handlebars with their heads pulled in low so as to make themselves more aerodynamic.

"Ready!" Charlie yelled. "Set!" He paused, giving one more glance and smirk to his sister.

"GO!" yelled Lizzie, before Charlie had a chance, and she burst out of her starting position like she'd been shot from a cannon, gaining the early lead.

Soon the two teenagers were speeding on the jet-powered flying motor bikes into a forest of wimberlies with snow like seedlings falling all around.

THE END

92471251R00145

Made in the USA
Columbia, SC
01 April 2018